FAÇADE *of* Shadows

SECOND EDITION

Rick Chiantaretto

ISBN-First Edition: 978-1589823525
ISBN-This Edition (2): 978-1-940748-03-0

First Edition, October 2006 by Bedside Books
This Edition (2), June 2014 by Orenda Press

Published by Orenda Press

Cover Design by Eden Crane Design
Production Management by Orenda Press

Publisher's Note: *This is a work of fiction. Names, characters, places, and incidents either are the product of the author's imagination, or are used fictitiously, and any resemblance to actual persons, living or dead, events, or locales is entirely coincidental.*

Chiantaretto, Rick, Façade of Shadows

There can be no darkness
except in the absence of light.

For my mom
who never believed in vampires,
but always believed in me.

Printed in the USA
This Edition, June 2014

PROLOGUE

Julian loved the rain; not because it cleansed the world but because it made everyone's life as dismal and gray as the clouds above, as gray as his soul always felt. The only problem with bad weather was that not many people would go out on such a night, and Julian could feel his lust for blood growing intensely. Unlike the others, he hated that feeling. Killing an innocent person or turning them into one like *him* was not something from which he gathered pleasure. Yet, the rules bound him.

Those very rules caused Julian to felt a rush of horror when he saw a shadow flash across his path on its way to the other side of the street. Yet, mixed with the disgust he felt for what he was about to do, he also received a distinct sort of satisfaction. He crossed the desolate road and saw a young woman tightly clutching her umbrella. He watched her for a while, curious as to why she would be out on such a rainy night. For a moment, he even thought he caught a glimpse of a smile on her face. This made him pause, and he decided to follow and observe her silently in the darkness.

Julian ducked into the shadowed tree line as the headlights of a large bus cast beams of light through the misty night. The woman stopped and turned as the bus slowly came to a halt. As the doors swung open, a dark man stepped into the awaiting arms of the woman, and as he kissed her, she dropped her umbrella and forgot about the rain.

Julian knew that he couldn't kill her. He didn't want his last kill to contradict all that he had worked for, to contradict the very reason he was out tonight. He wanted to get it over with, but wanted to do so by adding just another nameless, faceless person to those he had killed. He didn't want to add to his tally a face that smiled with such happiness.

This was why he felt tormented when another woman stepped off the bus. She was downtrodden, carried no suitcases or bags, and had dark hair that dripped like tears around her thin face. She walked slowly and aimlessly. Julian thought it seemed that if she were forced to choose between her dim existence and death, she would choose the latter—but perhaps he was merely justifying the heinous act he was about to commit. Reluctantly he approached her from behind, careful not to make a sound, and quickly covered her mouth with his gloved hand. As she struggled to resist his firm grip, he pressed his teeth deeply into her neck. The thick warmth immediately flowed into his mouth— how he loathed it! Next came the worst part: making her choose. He exposed his wrist to her and gave the

2

ultimatum that he had received three long years ago, "Drink or die!" As he suspected, she chose the latter, and Julian was satisfied that one less monster like himself would be doomed to roam the world.

Julian had just committed an act that always brought back another horrible memory. It had been a cold night, he remembered, but that was why he had decided to take a walk. He had used the cold night air as a convenient excuse to hold her closer. They had been walking along the shore of a man-made lake in the center of a park—he couldn't remember where—but even now he could clearly envision the moonlight reflecting off the calm ripples the wind made in the water. Her name was Fantasy, and to him, she had come from a fantasy. He had been looking forward to that night; he had wanted to prove that he and his love were fated to be together for eternity. A black velvet box had weighed down his pocket, concealing a bright diamond ring, a ring that Julian planned to place on her finger and then promise his love to her forever.

That same love was why he had chosen to live in the miserable existence that he had suffered ever since.

Suddenly, in Julian's fractured memory, she was screaming under some inhuman beast, her eyes looking at Julian, crying out to him. She was only feet away, but another beast was already on him, and the beast was strong. Fantasy and he fought the beasts, but it seemed that no human strength was great enough to lift the creature off his body.

Julian recalled strange, chiseled teeth as they moved toward his neck bringing a cold, sharp pain, as if two icicles had pierced deep into his flesh. Then, the monster spoke to him, "Drink from me and serve my master, or die. Choose quickly!"

Julian, terribly afraid of death, understood what the beast wanted him to do. He sunk his teeth into the exposed wrist and drank with horror from the throbbing vein. He experienced an immediate sensation of falling. As he looked over for his love, he saw her take her last breath.

Once again, as he always forced himself to do during these flashbacks, he shook the memory from his mind and focused on the task at hand. The ring he had carried for his beloved on that night long ago, now hung from a thin twine around his neck and seemed to burn into his chest as penance for each life he took or forever condemned to an eternity of living death. The reason he came out tonight was to die, to reunite with his love in that great afterlife that she used to call *heaven*. He wasn't afraid of death anymore; he had already tasted it.

He had considered driving a stake into his own heart, but remembered that death as a vampire resulted in eternal purgatory, where the demons even now claimed his soul. Instead, Julian chose to attempt redemption. His task in venturing forth tonight was to look for the legendary slayer. It was said that the slayer had the power to conjure the Protector and his powerful book, *The Book of Amun-Ra*. This book, named after and authored by Egypt's two most powerful gods, contained spells that, according to myth, could weaken the grasp of the demons that controlled a vampire's tortured existence and return its soul to the body from which it was taken.

Julian walked on, pushing aside the events of the evening, knowing that on this night, the slayer would be in search of those who kill relentlessly, in search of those who become so hungry for blood that they couldn't resist the desire to venture out and momentarily quench their thirst. Julian knew she was searching for him. His only hope was to find her first.

"Excuse me," a female voice said firmly behind him. He turned slowly as she spoke, the confidence in her voice growing, "I saw you kill that woman."

Julian glared.

"I know what would go well with that meal," she said sarcastically. "A nice juicy stake!"

Her hand moved quickly for his chest, but Julian reacted with the animal-like reflexes that the bizarre condition of vampirism allotted him. He grabbed her wrist and squeezed until the thud of the wooden stake she had attempted to stab him with made a soft splashing noise in a nearby puddle.

"No one appreciates a good joke anymore," she said, glancing at the floating stake.

"Please…" was all Julian could get out before the girl's foot caught him full-throttle on the chin, sending him sprawling backward to the ground. The girl quickly reclaimed the stake and positioned herself for another attack.

Julian suppressed his desire for revenge and spoke softly, the now pouring rain blurring his vision. "Please," he said. "I need your help."

A quizzical look crossed the girl's face. Julian was

sure this was the first time a vampire had asked for her help.

"I think I know how I can help you," she finally answered.

"You do?" Julian asked.

"Yes. I'll help you straight into the afterlife," she said, taking an aggressive step closer.

"No, please," he stuttered. "Don't come any closer." He was amazed when she listened.

"Just don't move," she ordered. "And maybe I'll hear you out."

"Agreed," Julian answered, holding up his hands in a sign of resignation. "Allow me to explain. My name is Julian, and I…"

"Dispense with the pleasantries and don't beat around the bush. It's probably not for the best."

"I figure if I don't explain, you'll kill me."

"I'll probably do that anyway. I suggest you continue, and get to the point!"

He nodded. "About three years ago I was bitten, along with my soul-mate. I figured that any life with her was better than no life at all, so I chose *this*. Obviously she felt differently because she chose to die. Back then, I didn't believe in heaven; I didn't know what death was like. Now I've experienced it. I've been to purgatory. I know there must be a heaven because when I looked for Fantasy in purgatory, she wasn't there. If life continues somewhere, she must have gone elsewhere…" he trailed off.

Julian was astounded that the slayer was listening intently. Though she had not relaxed her stance, her voice was softer when she spoke, "So, what can *I* do?"

Julian explained, "It is rumored that you can contact the Protector, and I believe he can set me free."

"Contacting the Protector is not as easy as picking up a phone. He is a supreme being, an embodiment of all good," she said.

"Then you can do it?"

"Why would I help *you*?"

"Haven't *you* ever made a mistake?" Julian asked.

"Not one like *that*. Besides, the Protector is against evil, vampires, demons, and everything else that has Satan for a friend, get it? He will kill you the moment he sees you, like I should have done already."

"I am told he can see into the hearts of… people, and he will see my intent. It is my risk to take, and I beg you to let me take it," Julian countered.

"He can see into the hearts of people, not vampires."

"You said yourself he is a supreme being; he will see into my heart."

"How can you prove to me that this isn't some sort of elaborate vampire trap? A slayer's blood is supposedly delectable, or so I've heard."

"Have you ever loved?" he asked.

"Huh?"

"Have you ever loved someone?"

"…Yes."

"Prove it."

She walked up to him. Julian prepared for a strike but instead the only thing thrust at him was her outstretched hand. "I'm Cynthia," she said, "and I can't believe I am going to do this for a vampire."

***

Julian marveled at all the candles that flickered around the room. He thought about counting them, but knew that the sea of tiny flames would only mesmerize him. There were other objects—vials of colored sand were scattered throughout the room, and at the front was a table covered with more sand, whiter and more pure than anything he had ever seen before. He wondered what each object represented.

"Sit here," Cynthia commanded, gesturing toward a triangle etched deeply into the cement floor. "Don't breathe so hard. If one of these candles goes out, the result could be catastrophic."

Cynthia walked to the table and, using her fingertips, drew two triangles in the sand that crossed at the center like an hourglass. She then defined the lines with the colored sand from around the room. Red, green, blue, and yellow now violated the white sand's purity. She took the last vile of black sand and approached him. "Don't bite me," she said sarcastically.

Julian couldn't resist a smile as she sat next to him. "I don't understand all of this," he said, becoming instantly serious.

"Well," she started, "I don't get it all either. I do know that the candles represent light and truth—there are exactly 50,000 of them." She caught the amazement in his eyes. "If you think that's incredible, get this: they all light themselves. The white sand represents the

Protector, perfect and pure. He is Horus, the Egyptian god, the god that injured his uncle Set. The colored sand represents you, stained with the evils of this world. You see, the white sand can encompass the evil and make it pure again. The black sand in this vial represents me. I am purity and evil combined in all colors. I'm good, because I fight for good, but I am nowhere close to perfection."

Julian sat silently in awe for a long moment while Cynthia seemed to meditate on the words she had just spoken. Finally, he became impatient and asked, "So what's next?"

Cynthia snapped back into reality, sarcastically rolled her eyes, and nodded her head.

She pulled the crystal lid off the vial she held and poured two piles from it, one in front of her and the other in front of Julian. She then carefully removed a handful from the remaining sand and threw it in a complete circle around them. The flames of the candles caught each particle, making the whole room appear to burst into flame. It was beautiful; the orange light dancing around them made Julian feel invincible. Then the light show ceased abruptly; the candle flames wavered into oblivion and the colored sand on the table returned to the pure white that it had been before Cynthia began the strange ritual.

"I don't think it worked," Julian said, troubled.

"I always answer a slayer's call," a voice resounded throughout the room as a figure stepped from the shadows. He carried with him a large book that glistened gold in the moonlight streaming from a nearby window. His voice, like a mellifluous choir, filled the room. He snapped his fingers, and all of the candles again erupted into flame. "I hate the dark," he stated petulantly.

"Sir," Julian began, but when the Protector raised his hand, the majestic gesture seemed to silence the entire world.

"I know why you have persuaded this slayer to contact me," he spoke. "You wouldn't be standing here if I thought your actions were in mockery of me, or of her." The being continued, "I know your desires, your fears, your hatred... and your love. You must understand, however, that returning a soul to a previous status is no easy matter. It requires a perfected power and much energy. You chose this life. Why should I exhaust myself to end it?"

Julian balked at speaking the truth he had so long denied to himself. Finally he burst out, "Because I didn't know; I didn't know which choice she was going to make! I didn't know if she would choose life or death. I didn't consider the consequences. I only wanted to be with her, to save her and to save myself. Then she was gone, and I didn't realize how much I loved her until she was no longer at my side."

The Protector paused, lost in thought. "You have impressed me. Finally you speak the truth. For that, you shall be rewarded. Look!" he commanded, motioning to the window.

Julian looked, his fear withering away as inexplicable joy took its place. In the sky, Julian saw trillions of stars. Then, he saw one star dash across the sky, then another, and another. Soon hundreds came at a time, assembling at a single point directly in front of him. He was embraced by blinding yet warm light and felt the strange sensation of falling. When he was able to regain his footing, he stood facing a figure that was more beautiful than he remembered. Fantasy touched his face as tears of joy rolled down her cheeks.

"Hi there," she said in a whisper.

***

"So where did you send him?" Cynthia asked the Protector.

"To his fantasy," he replied, with a satisfied smile at the clever play on words.

Cynthia looked at Julian, who lay unconscious and dreaming on the floor. "Wasn't his heart pure enough?" she asked.

"Of course, my friend," he answered, "but he *is* a vampire, and I have rules too. I cannot return a life that he willingly chose; I cannot undo what was done."

"Must *I*?" Cynthia asked. "Won't you?"

"It is your job," he responded.

Cynthia looked at Julian once more; he looked so peaceful. She tore her eyes away from his face, took the stake from the Protector's outstretched hand, and thrust it into Julian's heart.

CHAPTER ONE

It was always the same. She sat at a long wooden table with people who were very powerful. She could feel their power as though she were one of them. She wore a flowing white dress, and she felt the weight of a tiara resting on her head. She turned her gaze to her left and found herself sitting at the right hand of a man dressed in royal robes. He was laughing at a joke that she didn't hear. He raised a glass to his lips and took a large swig of ale. She could smell alcohol in the air around her. It was sickening. She knew who he was: he was Osiris, the god of Egypt—her husband. She realized she had also had a little too much to drink.

Then came trouble. She knew it would come, but it was almost as though she had forgotten. Still, she did remember that Set, the brother of Osiris, coveted the throne, and he coveted her as well. His greatest desire was power over the living world, and he was willing to take any action to attain that power.

Now, as a powerless bystander, she watched

intently. Everything was so vivid. She knew, but couldn't do anything about it, almost as if she couldn't speak or move. If she could just warn him—but she couldn't utter a sound. It was literally impossible to tell her husband that Set had created the box, cursed it, used his power over the dead, and that he was now going to issue a challenge, a challenge made under the pretense of drunken mirth.

The challenge that Set offered Osiris was to escape from the box. She watched as her foolish love entered what would become his coffin. The lid closed, and Set quickly poured molten lead into the box. Osiris tried to escape, but the evil magic held him bound.

She knew that he would die. She watched as Set commanded his servants to pick up the box and throw it into the Nile. She tried to run to her husband, but before she could get her feet to move she became confused again. It always ended here. She wanted to know what happened. She fought to try to remain in the vision, to save her husband. She loved him... she loved him.

***

The sky was dark and poured rain. The journey from Seattle to their destination took less than two days, but seemed much longer. Some played cards while others just watched the wind outside the bus windows as it rippled through the trees, bending the mighty plants to its greater power. Some slept to the sound of the rain pelting the windows of their dreams. Finally, on a late Tuesday afternoon, the driver turned and slowed to a stop.

Dominique woke to the sound of squeaking brakes, a sound that grated on her nerves. She despised moments like this that aggravated her heightened senses. Her senses were the most acute when she first woke up, as though they had stored power overnight. *It's always the same,* she thought. This strange dream had started over a month ago. The first time she dreamt it, she didn't understand what was going on, but as the dream repeated, she remembered it from beginning to end. Whenever the dream began she knew that the man sitting to her left would die while she would participate as a mere spectator, powerless to alter its outcome. That was the most frustrating part. Dominique had always sensed that she had been born to help people. Yet, in this dream, she was repeatedly forced to watch herself do nothing. The recurring dream had become more like a memory to her, one she wished she didn't have to relive.

The driver shifted stiffly in his seat, turning toward the passengers. The door to the bus opened, and with a grunt and a gesture, he commanded them out. The other passengers who had been sitting behind Dominique stood, some with luggage in hand, and glared at her rudely, as if saying, "Hurry up; get up! We're here." The driver had the same look in his eye. He had a schedule to keep.

Dominique stood slowly, taking a bit of extra time to stretch, just to annoy the driver and the other passengers. She didn't like being told what to do.

Dominique enjoyed being sarcastic, a little rude, and why shouldn't she? She always got away with it. She stepped off the bus into the rain, her shoe splashing in a small puddle. She was surprised to see that instead of a bus station, two small buildings stood side by side. A blinking sign on one offered weary travelers two options: rent a room or rent one of two junked, midsized cars to escape the dreary scene. The second building was a public bathroom. She hated it here already.

"Welcome to Pleasant Grove, Utah," Dominique muttered under her breath. She looked around and found the streets deserted. The other travelers seemed to have vanished into the rain. The bus driver glanced awkwardly at her, pausing for a moment as if to consider if she would be safe alone. He must have made up his mind quickly, because he shut the door and pulled noisily away, leaving her in a cloud of exhaust. There were no houses in sight, just a forest of trees that loomed on the sides of the road.

She walked a while, and then turned down one of the neighboring streets hoping to find whomever it was she was supposed to meet, if anyone. That was the problem. Dominique wasn't sure who she was supposed to be looking for; all she knew was that she was called here. Her watcher, a guide to a slayer, sent her here with his blessing and nothing more. He wouldn't even discuss the reason she was to leave, or when she would return. This was awkward. Up to this point Dominique had never been out of her hometown of Seattle.

Eventually, she retraced her steps back to the so-called bus terminal. At least the rain had stopped, and three people—two men and a petite girl—stood looking at her, as though they were waiting for her.

The group seemed out of place. Standing in the gloomy world, these three people seemed illuminated with power. A light radiated from them, a light separate from the light that streamed from the parted clouds. Their power shone in the way they stood, firm and resolute, heads held high but not defiant.

Dominique's eyes scanned them quickly as she walked toward them. "Wow, children of the corn!" she muttered to herself to calm her rising nerves. There was something special about one of them in particular, she noticed, immediately dismissing the importance of the other two in favor of the one. The power, the light of the group, emanated from him.

She walked swiftly in his direction, her eyes fixed. The wind blew her dark blond hair into her face. As she approached, the only female member of the group, an Asian girl no more than five feet tall, stepped forward with outstretched hands.

"Dominique, right?" she asked.

Dominique was much more interested in speaking to the one she considered to be the leader. She planned to ignore this girl completely, but as she brushed past her arm, she caught a faint spark in her compassionate eyes that made her stop and turn. She looked the girl over carefully; her slight frame seemed to be supported by an inner fire. Her silky hair curled gently under a powerful jaw. She carried herself with a poise that spoke of catlike agility.

"Another slayer. Great," Dominique said sarcastically, with a slight roll of her eyes. "I heard a rumor there might be two of us in the world."

"Sorry we're late. I'm Cynthia, by the way," the girl replied, ignoring Dominique's obvious lack of courtesy. She thrust her hand out again.

This time Dominique took it, surprised at Cynthia's firm grip. "Pleasure," she stated nonchalantly, realizing her mistake in judging this girl... woman... as unimportant.

"And that is James," Cynthia said.

Dominique spun, hoping to meet the glowing creature that she so desperately wanted to know. She tried to hide her disappointment and faked a smile when the other member of the group stepped forward.

"Nice to meet you," he uttered. "It was actually Cynthia's fault we weren't here on time; she had to fix her hair," he chuckled. "It seems she was hoping the new slayer would be of the opposite gender."

"Very funny, James," Cynthia sniped.

James smiled, and Dominique noticed that as he did so, her anxiety melted. She already liked him. His dark eyes were warm and matched his raven hair that was thrown about carelessly by the wind. His stance was more relaxed than Cynthia's had been, probably because he wasn't a slayer, but nonetheless, he looked prepared for anything. *Why was that?* Dominique wondered. *Why was it that this average young man looked as though he could take on a fleet of vampires?* She understood as her eyes fell to his chest, which boasted a small pendant, suspended by a thin black string around his neck.

"You into witchcraft?" Dominique asked, taking and twirling the pendant in her hand, inspecting it carefully. It was warm in her palm, burning with an inner fire that emanated not from the pendant, but from the bearer of it. James was powerful.

"Wicca," he answered softly, pulling the pendant away and tucking it into his shirt, somewhat annoyed at Dominique's disrespect.

Could he sense my thoughts? Dominique wondered. She shrugged. "It's kind of unique?"

"What?" James responded to her incoherent question.

"It's kind of unique, isn't it? A Tongan, in the middle of Pleasant Grove? I didn't think Utah would be so diverse."

James's mouth fell open in surprise at this slayer's contempt. "Cynthia isn't from American descent either. I've never considered myself exceptionally different."

"Just wondering if you ever felt that people were looking at you differently."

"If they are, it's not because of my race," he stated, a little annoyed. "You should go to West Valley, and then *you'll* feel in the minority. I would think you'd understand, being a slayer and all. Don't people look at *you* differently?"

Dominique considered. "I like that you are as straightforward as I am."

"Perhaps one day I'll teach you a little tact."

Dominique grinned, making a mental note that she could trust James.

"And you've already been introduced to him… at

least by reputation," Cynthia said.

James stepped to the side, revealing the third member of the small group.

"Finally," Dominique whispered, stepping forward to meet him. After a moment of contemplation she stated, "We have been introduced. Hello, Horus."

The face she was looking at was familiar, even though she had seen it only a few times before. His strong facial features were as unmistakable as his stern eyes, yet his young face had been softened, almost to the point of being unrecognizable.

"It's good to see you again. It's been a very long time. You look different. The last time I saw you, you seemed more... supreme. Look at your clothes! Did your mother dress you?"

He gave her a sharp look, crossed his arms, and stated, "I have been living as a mortal."

"And are we happy about that?" Dominique chuckled mockingly.

"Quite," he sighed, and with a slump of his shoulders continued, "but it bores me. I will explain in further detail at a later time, in another place."

"You even sound mortal. What happened to your *many voices of flowing waters*?" Dominique stated with amusement. "And why did you ask me to come to this godforsaken place anyway?"

"Because that is exactly what it has become," he responded cautiously, starting to turn away from her. "Again, now is not the time; we are being watched. Let us discuss this more formally... and in a more formal place."

"I'm not one for formalities, or rushing. You, however, always seem to be on some almighty schedule."

"Earth is on a schedule, Dominique," he stated, his face becoming angered at her perpetual disrespect, "and that schedule foretells its end. You're an intelligent, albeit somewhat irritating human, and a chosen one at that. I thought you would have figured that out by now."

"I don't live by anyone's schedule," Dominique snapped, turning her back to the group with folded arms.

He remained perfectly serene, but his voice commanded the heavens as he replied, "You do now."

A silent hush blanketed the world. The birds in the trees ended their songs. The wind ceased as a crack of thunder shattered the silence. A damp smell returned to the air as the clouds grew heavier and darker.

After a long pause, Cynthia stated as humbly as possible, "Perhaps we should be headed back to my place. It looks like more rain."

The Protector nodded his head once slowly, a twinkle of light flickering across his eyes as he smiled. To Cynthia the look hinted of compassion and amusement. This was going to be difficult, but all was necessary.

Meanwhile, Cynthia had her own questions about why another slayer needed to be brought in to aid her in her own domain. After meeting this stranger and catching the look in the Protector's eye, she realized it was for his good as well as hers. He needed a challenge, and from the looks of things, he would definitely have one now. The thoughts that now disturbed Cynthia were simple: *Was it Dominique that would cause the challenge, or did the Protector see something in the future that scared him enough to call another slayer? The Protector feared nothing; he couldn't. His power was too great. Or was it?* That thought made Cynthia shudder as the four of them walked into the trees.

CHAPTER TWO

"He has brought in another slayer," a hushed voice whispered. "She is more powerful than the first, but more rebellious. She angered him."

"I see no reason why we should not continue," said another, stronger voice. "We have been working under Horus's nose, and neither he nor the first slayer has had the power to hinder our progress. One more girl? I'm not too worried. Did you speak to the witches?"

"They are working as fast as they can," said the first.

"It is not fast enough. Speed them up."

"They say the spell is delicate. Perfection is key."

"Give them whatever they want. It must be finished."

A distinct pause followed. "The first wishes for only one thing…"

"Which is?"

"Me, Father."

"Then give yourself completely."

***

"Cheese in a can, the best thing ever invented," Dominique declared as she rummaged through Cynthia's fridge, shoving aside the steamed vegetables and meatloaf leftovers. The rest of the group sat on the couch in the living room, resting comfortably, chuckling quietly to themselves.

"I don't know why I'm so hungry," Dominique said, returning with a can of sharp cheddar and a box of Ritz crackers. "Long trip I guess. Would you like any… eh, what do they call you here anyway?" she asked, diving into the couch, sprawling with one leg hanging over the arm of the flowered upholstery. "I mean, you can't very well go by 'Majestic One' now can you?"

"I am Horus," he answered.

"I know your real name," Dominique continued, "but if you go by Horus the kids at school will make fun of you."

He looked at her with a half smile on his face. "Rick," he replied quickly with a glare. "While here, I go by Rick."

Dominique laughed, as he knew she would, "Rick!" she cried. "Where did you come up with that?"

His look changed, silencing her. "The Powers That Be assigned it to me. It has significant meaning to them, as it should to you."

"Why?"

"Rick means king, one who watches, cares for; a powerful ruler. I oversee. The big picture is not hidden from me. As Isaiah said, 'But they that wait upon the

Lord shall renew their strength; they shall mount up with wings as eagles.' I am an angel mounted up; an eagle who is to set off a chain of events, provided all goes well."

"All right, I'll give you that. It's just weird is all, you having such a… common name. It's a bit ironic," she stated while stuffing crackers into her mouth, still half laughing. She shifted her weight. "Hey, since this is the first time I've had the opportunity to speak to a, well, you know, angel of sorts, maybe you could answer a few questions for me."

Rick sighed, "Oh, here we go. Haven't you tried prayer?"

"Very funny," Dominique replied. "Come on, just one question."

Rick glared at her, "The universe has many secrets that I cannot reveal."

"It isn't a secret-revealing type of question. Can't you just answer me one *age-old* question?"

"Ask it. We'll see if I can answer, or if fate has already planned an experience for you to *learn* the answer."

"Why do bad things happen to good people?" Dominique asked.

Rick glared at her with derision. "Typical. You are asking me about the nature of God?"

"I dunno, seems like a simple question to me. I'm asking you about whoever is in charge."

"God is in charge. Below him are his servants like the Powers That Be. They control fate. Fate controls them. They control me… sort of. I can't explain it any better than that for the mortal mind. Dominique, God, as you see him, has granted each of us one particular gift. He gives it freely to all. This is a gift you will learn much about. The gift is not love, not power, not blessings. Do you know what that gift is?"

"Suppose not."

Rick's face fell in disappointment. "Okay, Cynthia? Can you help her out, please?"

"Agency," Cynthia chimed.

Rick beamed, "That's why you're my favorite."

"Agency?" Dominique repeated.

"Yes," Rick continued. "Let me try to explain it to you. Here on this earth everyone has the power to choose. Neither God, nor any of his servants, will interfere with your personal choice. It is how the world works. God chooses freely, and as such, he has chosen to give that gift to you as well. Yet, the consequences of our choices are not ours to choose. Each choice has a consequence and cannot be undone. God has said that if you choose to be a vampire, for instance, you will remain forever in a purgatory-like state. Choose it if you will, but there is no turning back. You cannot choose to become a vampire only to change your mind later. Does that answer your question?"

"No, all you did was tell me about choice. What does that have to do with bad things happening to good people?"

Rick gave James a look that communicated his disdain. "All right, Dominique, let me explain it in terms that not even you can misunderstand. Assume for a moment, that James here decided right now to pull out a gun and shoot the living daylights out of you. Would I be able to stop that?"

"I'd sure hope so."

"Well, that's your hope. I would do nothing."

"What? You're here to protect the world, and you'd let him shoot me?"

"I'm here to protect the world from consequences it didn't choose. Now you didn't choose in this example to be shot, but James chose to shoot you. Assume that James then dies, and he stands on the last day to be judged. His judges will then look at him and ask, 'Why did you shoot Dominique?' He would then be condemned for his action and cast out. Now, assume for a moment, that I did stop James from shooting you. The last day comes, and James's judge stands before him. Could James be condemned for shooting you if it never really happened? Even if it was James's intent to kill you? How would the judges be able to condemn James if he used the defense that he never really shot you? No crime took place, so James would be innocent. You see Dominique, if bad things didn't happen to good people, there could be no judgment."

"I just think the bad people should kill each other."

"Then there would be no opposition, no good versus evil, and as such, no judgment."

Dominique laughed. "So the reason bad things happen to good people is because evil has made a choice, and you can't take away its agency."

"Exactly. You will learn that for yourself eventually. Hopefully this bit of knowledge will help you on your quest."

"Speaking of," Dominique saw her moment, "can you tell me what my purpose here is?"

This time it was Rick who laughed. "Now you've asked for two of the universe's secrets! But don't worry, you will meet *her* tomorrow."

"I *really* don't like the way you said that," Dominique replied.

He continued to smile.

After a pause, Dominique observed casually, "Not to change the subject or anything, but where exactly are you living? If you are living as a teenager you've gotta learn to party like one, and sooner or later someone is going to want to come over to hang out or something."

"As far as anyone knows, I live here with Cynthia... a foster brother of sorts," he replied.

"You live here, with her? Well I bet that puts a damper on any relationships you—"

Rick interrupted, "Unlike some people, Dominique, I am not here to mate."

"Wow, a sense of humor and everything," Dominique noted. "Impressive. Does that come with the whole mortal-teenage-package thing, or did you haffta pay extra?"

The smile returned to his face while the others struggled not to laugh.

"Dominique," Cynthia broke in, "you eh... have some cheese," she said with a chuckle, pointing to the corner of Dominique's mouth.

Dominique slapped her hand to her lips and wiped with one overzealous swipe. "What about you, James? Don't you ever go home?"

James smiled pitifully, trying to remain happy. He failed, the smile faded and the twinkle in his eye darkened to blackness. His face was blank as he explained, "My mother died giving birth to me. I also lost my father. He was... uh... had a fishing accident, just over five years ago. He loved to fish."

The room fell silent.

"I'm sorry," Dominique stated.

James shrugged, "We weren't that close."

"You weren't?" Cynthia asked.

"Well... I tell myself we weren't."

Rick looked at James with surprise. "Your father loved you very much, and you loved him. During your childhood you two were inseparable. He was a master of the craft and had many powerful friends that even now influence your upbringing."

"How did you know that?" James questioned, "I never told you my father was a practicing warlock." Then, seeing the look in the Protector's eye, he asked quickly, "What do you know about the events surrounding my father's death?"

"What makes you inquire? What do *you* know about the events surrounding your father's death?"

James dodged the question by answering the first, "You have a look in your eye—the one you get when you know something, when you know something bad is about to happen."

"I always have that look when I am about to be beaten in chess by Cynthia." His eyes fell from James's. "She only plays me because I am the only person on earth she can beat."

"We just started the game!" Cynthia spouted, but with a grin and an agreeing nod.

"Yes, and I see glimpses of the future. No big deal; these mortal mind games are beneath me anyway," Rick said smiling, tipping his king in a sign of resignation. His smile then faded slowly, and a look replaced it that Dominique had seen before—worry.

"The sun is setting," she said, verbalizing his thoughts. The others had hardly noticed that the clock had been ticking for over three hours since Dominique's arrival. The sun was indeed gliding past the peaks of the western mountains into oblivion.

"Cynthia, I need you to patrol on the east side of town tonight. I will meet you there and give you further instruction," Rick said, becoming dreadfully serious. "James, I have noticed the awful stench of witchcraft afoot for approximately three days now, and the spell is souring. I need you to find out who, or what, is causing it. Do not attempt to solve it yourself. It is the most powerful spell I have perceived in ages. The power of its horror is as great as my peace, so be careful. Do not cast anything unless you speak with me first. Dominique, I want you to patrol the west side of town. There is a social gathering tonight at a club called Area 51, and I need you to make sure that the participants there remain safe. Vampires don't like crowds, but they will undoubtedly be lingering in the shadows, waiting for an unsuspecting reveler to wander off. Kill the vampires; we don't need any more to be born."

"I'm going to a rave?" Dominique asked. "Great!"

"I need you to stay and patrol until daybreak."

"Hello? Sleep!" Dominique protested.

"I promise you this: follow my guidelines and you will be astonished at how rested you feel in the morning; deny them, and you *will* be exhausted. Now is not the time to be flippant. Dark forces exist here that you have not yet begun to realize. I need you out all night eliminating as many of those forces as you possibly can. The vampires are building an army out there that no human can afford to underestimate. Imminent destruction of this town seems very real. Lives *will* be lost. You wanted to know why you were brought here? This is the reason: a war is brewing that will decide the fate of the earth, and it is now at our door."

Dominique rolled her eyes. "You make it sound like the king of the vampires himself has moved in next door!"

He looked at her apprehensively, shifting in his seat. His eyes burned into hers as he replied, "His name is Set."

"Set?" Dominique froze. "I've heard that name. He's been in my…"

"…dreams?" Rick finished.

"How did you know?" Dominique asked.

"I exercised my power to call you here. As a result, you are having flashbacks… memories. They will continue until you figure out why you are having them, or what warnings they hold for you."

With those words, the mountains became dark as the last ray of sunlight vanished, and the world was consumed by the unwelcoming hands of darkness.

CHAPTER THREE

His voice roared through the caverns, "Nannette, Melanie, Sara!"

Three shadows appeared at the jagged rock doorway. Small, hurried steps could be heard at the end of the great hall, like an echoing metronome keeping time for the underground. The shadows began to take form in the dim light, revealing three old women with sunken, haunting faces. However, an inherit beauty existed in those faces, as if their aged features gave them a mien of power and distinguished maturity.

"Master," they whispered in one hushed voice.

Set had his back turned to them. The hood on his flowing cape cast shadows over his expression. He turned toward them, his red eyes encased in small slits. His face looked more hideous in its relaxed state than in anger. The shadows fell over him, embracing him, and he moved in such a manner that he embraced the shadows as well. Two pillars of fire stood at each side of him with nothing to fuel them except the escaping breath of the underworld. The flames enhanced the darkness, causing shadow to define the corners and crevices of the cavern and the corners and crevices of Set's face. "Have you completed the task I have assigned to you?" he asked with a hiss.

They responded in a unified whisper, "Soon."

"What is taking so long?" he complained.

"Time."

"You will have it done by this week's end," he stated, rather than questioned.

The witches each flicked their heads in a dance that caused the darkness to creep across their own faces. "Perhaps," they intoned.

"Do you not remember how I helped you in your youth? I adopted you, trained you in the dark ways, and gave you the power you developed. You are only who you are today because of me! If I hadn't rescued you from that decrepit orphanage, you would have been separated, despised by all, grown old, and died five times over by now. I gave you immortality and even let you keep your imbecilic birth names! It is forever your duty to repay me. You *will* have it finished, or *I* will finish *you*."

"Do not threaten us. Do not judge us from your tower. For it is you, oh Dark One, who is finished without our power," they stated, lighting a small candle that cast an eerie light onto their sagging faces.

"I am finished either way. I have lived for thousands of years. This existence is beginning to tire me."

"Then you will cause a fate of death to come over your son, taking away his birthright? Don't you believe he is the One?" the witches asked.

Set smirked. "After having to work with you three, I wonder if he is worth my effort."

"Well then, Father, who would keep you company in your old age?" a strong voice echoed throughout the hall.

"All hail Lord Lucas, master of darkness, heir to the throne. We salute you, with three mighty tones," the witches chimed, extinguishing the small flame of the candle, which caused black smoke to rise toward the heavens.

"Silence, you old hags!" the voice boomed back at them. A figure materialized from a crevice in the rock high above the slate floor. The figure paused, remaining perched, balanced on the edge of the rocky ledge.

Set looked up and smiled. "Come, my son."

Lucas obeyed, jumping from the ledge and landed lightly, facing his father. He was in direct contrast with Set: his hair was blond, his eyes a pale blue. When he looked at someone, that person trustingly melted under his gaze. He learned to exploit this talent well and often manipulated people to get what he wanted. While his father used fear to control, Lucas acted as cool as ice but was not cold at heart. He was young, appearing to be around eighteen years of age, and was dressed accordingly in midnight cargo pants and a black shirt that was tight enough to outline his chiseled upper body.

He briefly met his father's eyes, only to then turn his

back on him to face the witches. He glided two steps forward and stood firmly in front of Melanie. He reached out taking her waist, pulling her gently into his body, enfolding her.

"Finish the necklace for me," he whispered into her ear. She studied him contemplatively and spoke for the first time without the others, "Aye, my Lord."

"Good," Lucas finished, releasing her quickly back to her sisters. She fell into the routine of unison instantly, as if she had never broken form. "Then go."

They nodded their heads, and the cavern was again filled with the sound of hurried steps as the witches' shadows faded into the rock.

When they were gone, the cavern was silent. The only sound was made by the burning flames licking voraciously at the oxygen. The room smelled of dampness and tasted stale. Lucas felt at home here. Set loved it.

Lucas remained with his back to his father, the silence lasting a moment longer before it was broken by slow footsteps approaching him from behind. A heavy arm encircled him. Long fingernails rested gently on his cheek.

"I would give my life for you, Lucas," Set stated.

"I know," Lucas said, turning to look at his father and pulling back his hood. The shadows that covered Set's face escaped for the safety of the cracks in the walls. Lucas bent, and kissed his father on the cheek.

"You are worried," Set stated.

"Somewhat," came the response.

"She will learn to care for you," Set continued.

"There is not a heart on this planet that could resist your beauty."

"That is not what I am worried about."

Set cocked his head and turned, the fire catching his red eyes, "Are you worried that you will not learn to care for her?"

"I already do; at least I am attracted to her. I believe it is her heart that attracts me so. It's warm… I saw her the other day and was filled with such a desire for her heart that I almost ripped it from her chest just to see what caused such warmth."

"You'd better resist that impulse, you inexperienced pup! If you are so attracted to her, then what's the problem?" Set sighed, turning his head back to catch his son's glare.

"Destroying something that good is… so evil."

"Would you have her destroy you then? Is that not equally as horrible?"

Lucas stared for a moment into his father's eyes, considering his question, then said, "Forgive me, Father. Of course you are correct. It is just that my feelings for her are difficult. If we were prophesied to be together, yet I do not love her… it seems so unnatural."

"You have been with many women; this one is only slightly different. Was it unnatural then? Do you not lust after her warmth? We are lustful creatures, Lucas. How is that unnatural?"

"It is the marriage part that bothers me."

"Ah," Set reprimanded, "and yet without the marriage, there is no point."

"There can still be an heir."

"No, Lucas. She must be accepted by our master in the ceremony of marriage. Satan himself must strike her and cause his power to fill her; otherwise she will give birth to something too weak. The whole fate of this world, and our ruling in it, rests on you, Lucas. After she bears you a son, slay her if you wish and continue with your life elsewhere. A few months of your time can save us all. Are you not willing to sacrifice so? You get a wife, you get a warm heart, you get her precious blood, and you get to fulfill all your lustful desires. The wedding may seem unnatural but…"

Lucas laughed, "…It is unnatural because we are *unnatural* creatures, Father."

"Only because we are supreme to nature."

Lucas pulled his glance away with a subtle expression of agreement, then turned and started to leave.

"Where are you going?" Set asked.

"I am hungry," Lucas responded.

"Watch yourself. The slayers are bound to be out tonight."

Lucas turned fiercely to his father, "Perhaps it is the slayers I am looking for."

Set pulled his hood back over his head allowing the shadows to return to his face, cocked his head, and sneered.

CHAPTER FOUR

Light trickled slowly over the mountaintops making Wednesday's eastern sky glow as if it were lit by fire. The sunrise remained dormant for a time, changing colors slowly until finally bursting over the horizon, causing the few remaining shadows to flee before it.

Dominique pushed open the door, almost falling into the house. The door's velocity ended abruptly after making a large dent where the handle pierced the wall. The sheetrock crumbled to the floor.

"Oops," Dominique said, receiving an unfriendly glance from the others.

Rick stood up, walked over to the punctured wall, and with one swipe of his hand repaired the damage.

"You lied to me," Dominique said.

"How so?" Rick asked.

"I have *never* been so exhausted in my life!" she screeched.

Rick turned and caught her gaze, and as he did, it was almost as if a spark was shared between them. "You're sure about that?"

"Yes! That had to have been the longest night ever! Does it really stay dark that long?" With a start, Dominique realized that she felt renewed, like she *had* had the best night's sleep ever. She smiled, "Oh, you're good."

"My power will have side effects. When you dream again, your memories will become more vivid. I know they seem real, but just remember that it isn't your life. It is just a dream."

Dominique gave him a look of confusion.

"Well then," he continued, "off to school."

Dominique's smile faded instantly and turned into a look of disgust. She made a sound that resembled a dying cat in three-hundred-degree heat. "I thought this was going to be a vacation."

"You will work harder this week than you have ever worked before. Remember that," he said with a grin.

"There's that look again…" Dominique said warily.

"What look is that?" he asked.

"The one that tells me I'm not going to like what you have planned for me," Dominique answered.

"Hope you have a number-two pencil," he replied.

***

The morning was still young when Dominique stepped out of the school's front office, surprised to find only Rick waiting for her. "Cynthia's home-

38

schooled, right? But where's James?"

"James goes to another school. He had a sort of *conflict* with one of the students here."

"Conflict? James?"

"People here tend to treat differently those who are different. James, practicing the craft, was not accepted."

Dominique didn't understand.

"Just do me a favor and try to fit in. If you don't, my whole plan could be foiled."

"Well, I'm registered. But you do realize it's the beginning of April, right? I got some questions as to why I was transferring so late in the year, and why I'm only signing up for the last two months. It's a good thing I'm creative… and a good liar."

She was turning to thrust her schedule at Rick when a blond-haired girl carrying three books, her nose buried in another, ran into Dominique at full force.

"Oomph," was the only sound that originated from the two bodies colliding, followed by heavy books hitting the floor.

Dominique shrieked, "Watch where you're going!"

"I'm sorry," a soft, yet defiant voice replied as the girl clamored to her knees, picking up her scattered possessions. She did it quickly, hardly taking the time to blink, and was off, her nose once again buried in her books.

"Geek!" Dominique cried out forcefully and turned back to face Rick.

He was attempting to repress a smile. "Can I see your schedule?" he asked.

Dominique handed it to him. He looked it over

thoughtfully. "Foods, home release, independent study, teacher's aide, practical English, painting, P.E...."

Dominique caught the disgust in his voice. "Well, I'm taking it easy my senior year, but unfortunately, English is required. Besides, I'm registering so late, they were the only classes left open," she chuckled nervously. "So when do I meet this 'chosen one' I'm here to rescue from the powers of hell?" she said, attempting to change the subject.

"You already have," he answered, handing her back her schedule. "And don't worry, these classes are open too."

The schedule was different now: advanced placement English, calculus, European history, and physics had replaced her previous slacker agenda.

"No, absolutely not! Her? How does *she* fit in?" Dominique cried, glaring at him.

"Hey," he answered, "you still have P.E. to look forward to. Have a good day at school. I'll see you at lunch. Oh... and make a new friend."

The bell echoed, and the hallways came alive with students moving frantically toward the classrooms. "You're late," Rick said calmly. He turned and disappeared into the crowd.

"Advanced placement English my..." Dominique trailed off, escaping to her classroom.

When she got there, she was glad to find another new student; she always felt more comfortable when she wasn't the only new one. The teacher seemed nice enough too. Dominique handed her the schedule to prove she was in the class and the teacher, anxious to begin, quickly made seating assignments for the two new students.

"Why don't you sit over there?" she suggested to Dominique, gesturing to a seat in the back corner. "And you can sit over here." The teacher pointed out a desk to the other student. Dominique took one step toward her seat and noticed... her. She was paying strict attention, even though the teacher wasn't saying anything that concerned her. Dominique wondered if she was taking notes on the new seating arrangement, as she feverishly moved her pencil. The other new student noticed the discomfort on Dominique's face.

"Don't worry," he said in a calm but confident tone, "I'll sit there, and you can have the one by the window."

Dominique felt a wave of relief. There was something about that girl that she just didn't like. "Thank you," she said to the student. She felt him brush her arm as he pushed past her; he felt like iron. This was the first time she had been able to get a good look at him. His arms were impressively muscular. He was dressed completely in black and looked back at her with stunning blue eyes.

"No, thank *you*," he said.

Maybe this class won't be so bad after all, Dominique thought, feeling herself melt under his gaze. He smiled, as if he knew what she was thinking.

"I'm Lucas, but most of my friends call me Luke," he said, pushing his hair out of his eyes with one hand and thrusting his other at her. She took it firmly.

"And may *I* call you Luke?"

That made his smile widen, "You may call me

anything you wish."

"Well, Luke, I'm Dominique," she stated with a sheepish grin, slightly embarrassed as she felt her cheeks turn warm.

"I know," he said, his cold hand penetrating the warmth of Dominique's own.

CHAPTER FIVE

The bell finally rang, releasing Dominique from her ambiguous paradise; one moment her mind was on Luke, the next, *that girl*. It was obvious now that this was the person whom the Protector wanted Dominique to become friends with—their schedules matched exactly, even the P.E.—but after spending most of the day together, Dominique didn't even know the girl's name. The good news was that Luke seemed to be on the same agenda also. Dominique could feel herself falling for him; he was so intriguing, mysterious, and those eyes were mesmerizing.

Now it was finally time for lunch, and Dominique forced herself to put him out of her mind. She was going to meet the Protector and needed to get into the frame of mind for business; Rick was always strictly business.

She burst through the door into the heavy noontime air and caught sight of him immediately. Rick was sitting under a large oak tree on the campus and talking, to *her*. He looked up, and noticing Dominique, motioned for her to come over, never missing a word of the conversation he was having. Dominique's feet obeyed, even though she didn't want them to, and she was soon standing next to Rick.

"I'd like to introduce you to Cassi," he said plainly.

"We've met," Cassi replied quickly, with a hint of contempt.

Dominique ignored her completely. "Can I speak to you... uh... Rick?"

"Sure," he said before turning to Cassi, "I'll be right back." He stood and walked with Dominique. Once they were out of Cassi's earshot, he continued, "I had hoped you two would become friends, Dominique. I *need* you to be friends."

"How long have you two been, you know, *friends*?" Dominique asked wryly.

"I know what you are implying, and no, I am not her *only* friend."

Dominique paused, waiting for him to continue. "Well?"

"She has many friends. Perhaps one day soon you will meet Debbie. She is Cassi's best friend. They have been friends since childhood."

"There's no day like the present. Where is she?"

"She hasn't been to school for the last few days. She seems to have disappeared just after Cassi invited her to her birthday party. Cassi isn't exactly sure where Debbie is, but her family is gone too. She lost a grandmother recently, and Cassi thinks her family went to rally around her grandfather, who is dealing with his loss rather poorly."

"So... do you know where she *really* is?" Dominique asked.

The Protector gave her a harsh look, "I assume she is where Cassi says she is."

"But you don't *know*?"

Rick slowed his step, "Why?"

"Well, it just seems a little strange to me. Cassi's best friend disappears about the time I show up here to protect her. Obviously the vamps are brewing up something. Best friends make great leverage."

"Leverage for what? The vampires can't make a move on Cassi without us knowing, and they can't exactly force her into anything. I'm Horus, remember? I have the power to change her back."

"If she doesn't *choose* to become a vampire."

"How else could she become one? Look, when I see Cassi worry about Debbie, I'll worry."

"How do you know she isn't worried?"

"We've been friends for over three years now. I can read her emotions, and I know when Cassi is lying to me about her feelings. I can tell when she is happy, when she is sad, and yes, even when she is worried. We have been friends for so long that we have developed something a little... more."

"She likes you, huh?"

"No," he said, hesitating wistfully, "we are just— very—good friends."

"So when she ran into me this morning, don't you think it was a little rude that she didn't even say hi? And why didn't you acknowledge her?"

"Because I interfered with fate by bringing you here. Let's assume for a moment that you never came to Pleasant Grove. Would you have been there for her to run into?"

"I suppose not. How could I have been there if I wasn't here?"

"Then if you weren't here, would she have run into anyone at all?"

"Perhaps she would have run into Luke. He seems to be around her all the time. Maybe she would have run into you."

"Why? Was it her fate to run into someone or no one at all?"

"How can you run into no one?"

"To that I answer: In fate's eyes, you were not supposed to be there. So now I propose the question, were you really there at all?"

"What? I'm not sure I understand. Why didn't she run into you then? You're changing the subject."

"I wasn't there, for her to see anyway," he replied, "which also explains why she didn't acknowledge me, and I didn't acknowledge her."

"But I saw you."

He turned to her and said, "You were the only one."

Dominique was silent, contemplating.

"You don't need to understand right now, or ever, for that matter. Fate is my realm of worry, not yours," he said. "I know, now, that you two will not become good friends as I had hoped. You gave up a seat today in first period, didn't you? Fate seems to have declared that seat the deciding factor in your friendship. *He* was not supposed to be there either, but now that he was, they will become friends. However, no one can cast blame. What is done is done. I need you to at least *tolerate* each other. You will be keeping an eye on her, or someone else will."

"I can handle that."

"Good."

***

Meanwhile, Cassi sat under the tree shaded from the April sun, watching her closest friend walk off with her newest enemy. She was lost in her own thoughts when a sudden high-pitched whistle shattered her daydreams. She looked toward the sound and saw the boy who had offered to sit by her. He was waving to her and had a soft smile touching his lips. He was almost invisible, hiding in the shadow that formed under an overhang. Holding out his hands, he invited her to him with a slight movement of his fingers. It was only the way he looked at her that made her consider meeting him there in the shadows.

She stood and walked out from her shady shelter into the blinding sun. She lost sight of him in the dark as the light glared in her eyes. She stumbled up the stairs, tripping over the top step, only to have Lucas catch her.

While steadying her, he took her hands in his own. "I understand you have a birthday coming up," he said with confidence.

"Yes," she answered quickly. "Friday. How did you know?"

"Eighteen, huh?" he continued, ignoring the question.

"Yeah," she answered, gaining courage.

He smiled. "Are you having a party?"

"I think some friends of mine are getting together. Why? Would you like to come?"

His smile widened.

"I'm sorry, that was a little presumptuous," Cassi said, backing away from him. She felt her face go red and turned to leave.

"I'd love to," he answered, remaining in the shadows.

She stopped in her tracks. The reply caught her off guard, but made her happy. She took one more step away, feeling good about herself, which seldom happened. She had already stepped into the light when the voice came again from the shadows, "Can I see you tonight?"

Cassi didn't turn around, just answered after some thought, "Nine o'clock."

She didn't wait for a reply, but walked back to the shade and comfort of her tree. When she turned back to see him again, her eyes had readjusted, and all she could see was darkness.

CHAPTER SIX

The shadows in the underground cavern intensified when Lucas entered. He found his father in the midst of a large group of other vampires. They parted, letting Lucas into the circle as he pushed past them. He knew he would find his father at the center of the group, but his father wasn't alone—a teenaged girl was with him. The vampires were tormenting her, playing silly games that Lucas found unnerving, but she remained unharmed. The room fell silent as Lucas looked at her, then at his father.

Set smiled back. "How was school, Son?" he asked with a smirk.

Lucas pulled his bag off his shoulder and threw it into one of the flaming pillars that provided the light in the cavern. The fire burned so hot that the bag caught fire instantly, and it hissed in the flames. Lucas's face was monstrous when he turned back to his father. "I

49

was trapped in that place until the sun set!" he snarled.

Set laughed. "You're experienced enough to walk in the light."

"No matter how experienced I get, it still burns, and the cavern is a long walk."

"Calm down, my son. Tonight we have reason to celebrate."

"Do enlighten me," Lucas growled with his fangs clenched.

Set walked out of the circle away from Lucas. The group of vampires parted to allow his passage. When he returned, he carried a small black velvet box in his pale hands. Lucas snatched it from him and pulled it open. His face softened when he peered at the sparkles that shined from the box. Resting inside was an elegant necklace. Suspended from a fine silver chain were two diamonds, one hanging from the other. The top diamond was black and appeared to absorb all light that fell upon it. The bottom diamond was crisp white, catching the light and reflecting it to cast small rainbows upon Lucas's forehead. The white diamond was suspended from the other gem by a delicate chain one inch in length.

"Who knew something so evil could be so beautiful," Lucas wondered aloud.

"Take a look at yourself," a female vampire cried from the crowd. "Are you not as equally beautiful as you are evil?"

A shout of agreement came from the population, but Lucas didn't seem to notice. He was captivated. "What is its purpose?"

"You see it now, my son. It holds you spellbound. It will help you win her heart. This way, she will never notice something is missing. She will never notice you don't love her."

Lucas clapped the box shut and fell out of his daze. "Such a powerful spell, for nothing but good looks? When was it finished?" he asked.

"The witches brought it in just after sunset," Set responded, "hence the celebration." He took the frightened girl harshly by her arm and thrust her at Lucas. "We have kept her fresh for you."

Lucas looked down and saw the fear in the eyes of the young woman. She had been crying for some time now, Lucas could tell. He then tore his stare from her, looked back at his father, and said, "What's this about? You've terrified her. Nah. I'm in the mood for Chinese." With that, he turned and began to leave the circle.

"Where are you going?" Set elevated his voice with such power that all turned to glare at Lucas. He met their stares defiantly, adjusted his collar, and responded, "I have a date."

***

Dominique and Cynthia sat together after school was over that day. Their friendship was different than anything either of them had experienced before. A special bond existed between them, a bond formed by the understanding gained through mutual experience. It was in this spirit that they were conversing about their lives, the call of being a slayer, what it meant, what they had learned, and what they feared. They both felt as though they could talk to each other in ways they had never been able to talk to anyone before.

"But I would like to know *where* they came from," Dominique stated coolly, "and honestly, how they came to be. The word *vampire* wasn't even used until the year 1047. Did vampires exist before that and there just wasn't a *word* for it?"

"I heard from somewhere that the first vampire was actually killed that year. I think he was killed in Scotland by some mysterious slayer. Rumor has it that one day this woman just rode into town right up to a chapel and hung him in the sunlight; the sun burned him, the hanging killed him. I don't really know if anyone knows how long he was around before that. Just look at Set; he's an Egyptian god turned bloodsucker. He's been around forever. How long has *he* been a vampire, do you think?"

"He wasn't one in my dream, that's for sure. Evil yes, but minus the fangs. I wonder what the time period of that dream is supposed to be. I don't remember seeing Rick in my dream, so it must have been before he was born. How old do you think Rick is, anyway?"

"Oh geez. He was around way before 1047. I don't really know his entire story either," Cynthia answered. "But I think he existed before the first vampire did."

"It's so confusing. I have no clue how the whole thing fits together. I don't even know when I was called to be a slayer. Was I born a slayer? Did Rick call me, or did some other messenger of God? Is Rick a messenger, an angel, or something else? Not to mention the whole fate-space, time-continuum, or whatever it is. It must have been nice, having Rick as a guide for these last few years. Lucky, I'd say. You can ask him any question you want."

Cynthia chuckled, "Oh no, I learned to stop asking him questions. Yes, it's true he's been watching over me for a while now, but only to get closer to Cassi. That is one thing I regret..."

Dominique noticed that Cynthia's face had fallen. "What? What do you regret?"

"Well," she continued, "Haven't you ever noticed how everyone in this house is friends with Cassi? I mean, James is practically her male confidant, Rick is her best friend in the world, and even you were *supposed* to become her friend."

"I don't follow. Just tell me what's on your mind."

"I guess fate even controls friendships. See, when we were younger, Cassi and I were best friends. She used to live next door here. We did everything together. Her parents work a lot, and when they weren't home, Cassi used to come over and hang out... you know, girl stuff."

"So what happened?"

"When Rick came, he needed someone to sacrifice their friendship with her so that he could fill that 'friendship spot' if you want to call it that. In order for a new friendship to be born, one had to die. That's all. One had to die..."

"Cynthia!" Dominique cried, climbing over to where she was sitting to give her a hug. "That's horrible.

Why would you let him do that?"

"It wasn't his fault. And I knew it. I knew that it would come down to that friendship in exchange for her life. So I watched as he became her new best friend. She gradually quit calling me, quit coming over... and now her life will be saved because of it. Rick needs to be close to Cassi. If he isn't, Cassi might make a choice that could be devastating."

"A choice that might be devastating? Sheesh, Cynthia, it seems like you should have had a choice. What has he been teaching you?"

"It was my choice. It really was." Then Cynthia brightened. "I remember a very firm lesson he gave me once about choice."

"Oh *this* should be good," Dominique stated, slumping back into the couch. "Go on."

"I had this *crazy* night once, when Rick had first come to Pleasant Grove. There was this vampire and, get this, he wanted his soul back."

"What?"

"Seriously. He was probably the noblest... well... most kind-hearted vampire I have ever seen. He wouldn't fight me. Instead, he talked about love, about life, and about second chances. He asked me to summon Rick to beg him to return his soul."

"He *what?*" Dominique laughed.

"It wasn't funny. The poor thing. I actually felt sorry for him."

"So did you do the whole candle with the sand, strange triangle thing?"

"Well, luckily for me, Rick had already set it up. He

told me to use it if I needed anything. It was during the preparation time, preparing the Cassi thing, while he was still at the putting-together-the-legend, jump-around-like-a-madman stage. He was gone a lot, and I didn't have another watcher."

"Did you do it? The summoning, I mean?"

"Yeah. If you ever need anything from Rick, I suggest buying the 50,000 candles. It's amazing."

"And what happened?"

"I don't really know. Rick told the vamp his heart was pure and that his desire would be granted. I still remember him asking Julian to look out the window."

"Julian?"

"That was the vampire's name. When Julian turned to look out the window, he fell to the floor muttering something, and even looked like he was crying."

"Did you just leave him there? Did he get his soul back?"

"No, he didn't. Rick looked at me and handed me a stake."

"You killed him after all that?"

Cynthia nodded. "I'll tell you what, I have never learned a more difficult lesson about choice. Rick told me that you can't go back on a decision. Once a decision is made for you, in your heart, even if you change your mind, there are still consequences. There was nothing Rick could do. I think he *wanted* to save Julian… Goodness, the memory is still so vivid in my mind."

A voice interrupted them. "It was a difficult night for us both, I'd say," Rick stated, walking into the room.

"And don't worry, Dominique, I wasn't eavesdropping. I heard the name Julian as I came in, and... Cynthia knew only one Julian—"

"I think I've figured it out, the witchcraft thing," James's calm voice sang as he came running down the stairway. "It wasn't in any book, but could possibly be bits and pieces of different spells." He carried four large books in his arms, all hardbound and blackened with age.

"Um, am I interrupting something?" he asked, noticing that all were staring at him.

"No, nothing," Rick responded. "Do show us."

James spilled the books across the coffee table and carefully turned to bookmarked pages in each of them. "See," he said, "this one talks about a power stronger than that found on earth, kind of like the Protector. This one boasts of an evil, with the power number 666." He shuffled around the pages. "Here. This spell binds a person, you know, so they can't do magic anymore. And this one, this one could be used to condense them all and force them into a talisman of sorts. It is this spell that I think you have been feeling—the refiner's fire. Something this powerful could only come from one place: the *Book of the Dead*."

"What's that?" Cynthia asked.

James hid his disgust. "The other side to *Amun-Ra*. Nature prides itself on balance. All good is counteracted by all evil, and vice-versa. The *Book of the Dead* is evil's bible, but it only heeds the call of very powerful witches."

Dominique and Cynthia stared at him, while the

Protector seemed lost in thought. Finally, with a quick jerking motion, he looked at the others and stated, "I concur."

"But the spell should have ended tonight, just after sunset," James said.

"So what was finished?" Cynthia chimed in. She glared at the Protector. "Is this something we have to worry about?"

He paused, "I believe our situation has become more dangerous, if that is what you are asking," the Protector replied. "Evil's task is nearing completion. Therefore, our tasks have just become more difficult. Dominique, you have met the person you have been brought here to defend. Now I feel it is time you learned why."

He stood, seeming agitated. He lifted his hands above his head and shouted, "*Amun-Ra!*" When his hands fell, they made a thunderous sound that shook the glass panes and rattled the walls. The room went piercingly white, as bright as the sun reflecting on a beach of alabaster sand. The sound of waves crashing against the barrier reef could be heard like some distant ocean that was growing closer until it swept them all into its infinite stretches. They were floating in the water, all of them, being enveloped by the lull of a warm summer day. It then fell dark for an instant before power returned to the lights in the house. When it was over the Protector was holding a magnificent golden book. He sat and began to thumb through the pages. "Come," he motioned to Dominique.

She obeyed willingly, in awe of what had just

transpired before her eyes. He pointed at a golden page. This was the first time Dominique had ever seen this marvel. She stared at the pages. They shone, having a unique way of capturing the light. Dominique couldn't read it. The markings on the pages looked Egyptian, hieroglyphics maybe. The strange words changed like flowing water; every instant something new appeared on the page that Dominique had not seen there a moment ago.

"Read," Rick commanded in almost a whisper. The air around her was still, the room silent. Even the world outside the window seemed to hush in the presence of this book, this guide to life.

"I can't," Dominique replied.

"Look harder," he demanded, moving his hand in a slight waving motion over the pages. Dominique stared, her mind falling deeper into the pages as if they were three-dimensional. Suddenly, she was in a room with nothing but words as the walls. She looked down and noticed her feet supported by two Egyptian symbols, gold in color, and far brighter than any others around her. Nothing existed beyond the symbols except the darkness of an endless abyss. With some courage, Dominique took a step to the next symbol, testing its firmness before trusting, watching its brightness grow as it began to support her weight. She almost felt the desire to jump from symbol to symbol, but figured the Protector would not be amused if she played around in his book. *In his book?* The thought surprised her. She gawked in a state of amusement and wonder as the walls around her continuously changed. Some symbols were lighter than others, bright and firm. Some were cold and dark, but blended with the light in perfect harmony. Dominique couldn't resist; she just had to try to reach out between two of the symbols, just to see what it felt like outside of this Egyptian room. As she reached, her hand turned cold. There was no air here; it was black, like space without stars—a black hole, matter collapsing into itself.

Her arm shuddered as the letter next to it shifted. She pulled her arm back into the room, just as the symbol slid over where her arm had been. The sliding symbol blended into the one next to it. The room was in a constant state of movement, but she realized that as she focused, words began to take shape, forming sentences, and eventually she read these words out loud:

> *A loud moaning cry heard from heaven to hell*
> *Escaping the aching lips of the just,*
> *A sorrowful groan from the one known as He*
> *When a cackle of chaos from the darkness fell.*

> *The eyes of mother, twinkling in the sky*
> *Her belly soon swells, and sealed is her fate.*
> *Her eyes grow dim, her heart hungry for blood,*
> *For the baby she bears is near its birth date.*

> *His coming will mark the hold of black roots,*
> *Its disease will spread to new heights of the sky,*
> *Blackness will blow and ripple the faith,*
> *One may make light prevail; many will try.*

A slayer be born, the world to defend,
Darkness and domination will soon after part.
The tyranny silenced as a new power purges,
Puts an end to the life of the Head through the heart.

The words then vanished, and the room went dark. When Dominique came to her senses again she was not in Cynthia's house. It was always the same. She sat at a long wooden table with people who were very powerful. She could feel their power as though she were one of them. She wore a flowing white dress, and she felt the weight of a tiara resting on her head. She turned her gaze to her left and found herself sitting at the right hand of a man dressed in royal robes. He was laughing at a joke that she didn't hear. He raised a glass to his lips and took a large swig of ale. She could smell alcohol in the air around her. It was sickening. She knew who he was: he was Osiris, the god of Egypt—her husband. She realized she had also had a little too much to drink.

Then came trouble. She knew it would come, but it was almost as though she had forgotten. Still, she did remember that Set, the brother of Osiris, coveted the throne, and he coveted her as well. His greatest desire was power over the living world, and he was willing to take any action to attain that power.

Now, as a powerless bystander, she watched intently. Everything was so vivid. She knew, but couldn't do anything about it, almost as if she couldn't speak or move. If she could just warn him—but she couldn't utter a sound. It was literally impossible to tell her husband that Set had created the box, cursed it, used his power over the dead, and that he was now going to issue a challenge, a challenge made under the pretense of drunken mirth.

The challenge that Set offered Osiris was to escape from the box. She watched as her foolish love entered what would become his coffin. The lid closed, and Set quickly poured molten lead into the box. Osiris tried to escape, but the evil magic held him bound.

She knew that he would die. She watched as Set commanded his servants to pick up the box and throw it into the Nile. She tried to run to her husband, but before she could get her feet to move she became confused again. It always ended here. She wanted to know what happened. She fought to try to remain in the vision, to save her husband. She loved him... she loved him.

***

A moment later, she returned to the silent glow of Cynthia's living room, awestruck, as if she had just come out of a trance. "That dream, always with that dream!"

"Worry about the dream later. Focus on the legend," Rick stated. "What did you understand from it?"

"I understand some," she said, full of questions, still dazed, "but the symbolism is confusing. What is this 'eyes in the sky' thing, and…"

"It is not required that you understand all. I don't understand it all yet either. Think about it. If you get any insight, discuss it with me. Fate has decreed what it has decreed, and all meaning will be unfolded to you as fate sees fit."

Dominique looked at Cynthia, who had tears in her eyes, then at James, who simply stared respectfully at the floor. "Well, you sure know how to bring down a party," Dominique stated with a slight chuckle.

***

Something or someone softly knocked on the heavy wooden door. Cassi bounded down the stairs of her split-level home trying not to appear, or sound, too desperate. The fact was, she wasn't, and she liked it that way. She had never needed anyone, but there was something about the way he looked at her that made her feel wanted, feel like more than just "that straight-A student."

She pulled the door open slowly, hoping to see Luke. Her wish was granted, as he was standing on her porch in his mysterious black clothing. She didn't know why she had doubted that he would come. Perhaps it was because, invitation or not, no one like him ever came to her house.

"I didn't think you would really come," Cassi stated, immediately releasing her doubts to him. She didn't know why, but she felt she could trust him.

He held up two cartons of Chinese take-out and smiled, "A guy's gotta eat."

"You can come in, if you'd like," Cassi said.

"Is that an official invitation to enter?" was his response.

Cassi paused, "Well aren't you polite."

"It's in my nature."

"Well, I officially invite you to enter then."

"Love to," he conveyed, entering the doorway. Cassi led him upstairs.

"It's quiet," he observed. "Where are your parents?"

"Called away on business. They won't be home until Monday."

"That means they'll miss your birthday?" Lucas questioned, trying to be gentle.

"Won't be the first time," Cassi responded with bitterness.

"Oh really? What do they do?"

"They're team drivers, going all over the country in a dirty semi-truck. They're *never* home. That's okay though. I guess all that matters is that they pay the bills, right? They really have no choice."

Lucas snorted, "That's no excuse."

"What about your family?" Cassi inquired, eager to change the subject. She really didn't have anything good to say about her family.

"Well, my father is always home. He hates leaving the… house. I guess you could say he's a real cave dweller. He never even goes out to eat anymore. I always end up bringing him something, running his errands, you know."

"How horrible. I've learned to love being alone. It gives me time to think."

"Don't get me wrong, I have time to myself. My father doesn't have much control over me. I'm often alone at the top of the mountains, in my room, by a lake, or by a river. When I want to be alone... well, let's just say I'm used to getting what I want."

"Ah, so you're an only child then," Cassi joked. "Me too."

Lucas chuckled. "In a way I am, I suppose. I'm the only biological son, but my father is a very powerful person. He has many followers; each of them is his child in a way."

"You make it sound like he's a priest or something."

"Yeah, something like that."

The conversation grew awkwardly silent. They sat quietly on the couch for a time before the silence got to Cassi, and she flipped the television on. Lucas opened his cartons of food. "I hope you like sesame chicken," he stated.

"I hope so too," Cassi responded. "I've never had it."

"Oh? You're missing out," he said, handing her a piece. She received it eagerly and took a small bite.

She looked at him with eyes wide. "That's good."

He chuckled.

"Hey, what happened to your cheek?" Cassi asked, taking another bite. "You've got some..."

Lucas swiped at his cheekbone, his hand coming down to reveal a spot of blood. "Heh, heh," he laughed uncomfortably. "I must have cut myself shaving."

Cassi's smile faded. The mood suddenly changed, becoming very wrong. The darkness seemed to come alive around her. Cassi wasn't sure what changed; he just wasn't looking at her now. The darkness strangled her. It was hard to breathe, as though the devil himself was in the room choking out the light. She snapped on the lamp next to the arm of the couch and watched intently as Lucas's pupils grew smaller in the light. "Why did you come here?"

He looked confused. "To see you, of course."

"Who put you up to this?" Cassi continued.

He looked hurt and put his hand over his heart feigning a mortal wound.

"Come on... no one like *you* ever comes to see someone like *me*."

Lucas grabbed Cassi by her arms and pinned her to the couch. Bending so close to her that she could feel his breath and feel the pressure of his chest against hers, he said in a low, passionate tone, "What is that supposed to mean? You are beautiful. Other people may not see it, but they misunderstand you. They don't see your heart, how warm it is." Then suddenly he stood, never taking his eyes off her. "Come with me, I'll show you."

His hand was outstretched toward hers, and although she took it somewhat reluctantly, he was able to coax her off the couch. They went to the bathroom where he flipped on the light and positioned her in front of the mirror. "Look at yourself."

She refused to obey and laughed nervously.

Gently, he took her hair in his hands and placed it, wrapping it around itself until it seemed suspended in air. It danced around her face in a way she had never seen it do before. Lucas took the dried flower decorations off the wall and wove them between her blond strands until they found new life and took root in

Cassi's hair. She looked into the mirror and didn't recognize her own face, realizing for the first time how beautiful she was, or, at least, had the potential to be. When he was finished, he rested his head on her shoulder and with a self-satisfied smile, watched her gawk at her own reflection.

"I told you," he whispered. "If you think that was magic, wait until you see what you look like tomorrow. I'll be here in the morning, five a.m."

With that, he turned, walked out of the bathroom, down the stairs, and out the door, closing it quietly behind him, leaving Cassi there alone, staring at her own reflection.

CHAPTER SEVEN

The moon shone brightly through Cassi's uncovered windows early that Thursday morning. It caused shadows to fall lightly across her face, illuminating her skin in a pale blue luster. Cassi turned, feeling warm, and reached to slap off her buzzing alarm clock. The instant she did, the doorbell rang.

Cassi jumped—he was fifteen minutes early! She threw her comforter around her mattress and pushed folds of material under her pillow, making her bed look made, but not neat. She brushed through her hair quickly to get out the tangles, alarmed at the static that caused strands to float in the air. She pulled open her bedroom door and bolted down the stairs, stubbing her toe on the corner of the stairway. By the time she finally opened the front door, she was worried he might be gone, but Luke was still there, dressed in opposite attire from the day before. Today he wore a white, short-sleeved fleece pullover and khaki pants that glowed in the moonlight. He carried two boxes in his arms.

"Well don't just stand there, invite me in," he chuckled. "I was getting a little impatient standing out here. Forget I was coming?"

"Oh," Cassi said, "Sorry. No. Come in. I'm still kind of asleep."

He looked her over. "You look good. Shall we?" He walked up the stairs hurriedly, not waiting to be led. When they reached the top, he motioned for her to sit on the couch. Cassi eagerly obeyed.

Luke handed her the boxes, then sat on the coffee table opposite her, their knees touching. Cassi just looked at the boxes cradled in her lap.

"Go ahead," Lucas said.

She pulled the lid off of the first box, revealing a short lilac top. It was simple, light, and of solid color. She looked at him and caught the smile that curled his lips. She grasped the other box. Inside was a pair of white drawstring pants. She stared at them, admiringly.

"Wait here, I'm going to go change," she said with almost a squeal.

He grinned in agreement. "I'm not going anywhere."

Cassi closed the door behind her and flipped the switch to her overhead light. It came on with blinding force. She stood in front of her mirrored closet doors and slipped the new clothing on. Both pieces fit perfectly and hugged her so comfortably that it seemed to her as if she were in an embrace that would never end. The shirt covered her stomach and fell just below the pants waistband. Everything was so simple, yet perfect. Lucas had obviously paid special attention to every detail. She finally took her eyes off her reflection and went back to the front room.

"Do something with my hair," she commanded Lucas.

He did what she asked, this time without going into the bathroom, this time with no mirror. It seemed to take twice as long as it had the night before. She felt him tug and pull at her blond strands as if a million tiny fingers were massaging her scalp. In this moment of bliss she forgot where she was, who she was, and almost fell asleep. She could imagine herself becoming whatever he wanted her to be. She was happy with that idea. Then he stopped, and Cassi reluctantly returned to reality.

He turned her to face him and kissed her cheek. "Go see."

Cassi walked into the bathroom. She was not afraid to look at her reflection, and when she did, she saw Eve. Her hair had no artificial pieces, yet it looked like leaves had been embedded in her locks. It fell carefully around her face and in front of one shoulder. It curled under at the tips, flowing beautifully. She smiled at her own reflection.

Luke came to the doorway, but didn't step in.

"Thank you," Cassi whispered.

"No," he said. "Thank *you*. Let's get to school."

"Why so early? It can't be after six o'clock in the morning," Cassi reminded him.

"I know. I just like to be there before sunrise."

She shrugged her shoulders, grabbed her jacket and book bag which waited conveniently by the stairway, and walked out the door. Lucas followed, closing the door with a soft click behind them. The early morning air was brisk with sudden breezes.

"It's gusty," Cassi said, almost skipping as she strolled down the sidewalk.

"Don't worry; there are plenty of places to run for warmth." With that and a smile, he took her hand and locked his fingers around hers.

"Are you going to be glued to me like this during school?" Cassi asked inquisitively.

"Only if you want me to be," was the response.

Cassi paused, nodded her head, and whispered to herself, "This is too good to be true."

Luke suddenly turned toward her, burning her with his eyes, "You read my thoughts just now."

They walked hand in hand, playing games with each other on their way to school in the dark. The passing cars brightened Luke's face, their headlights reflecting off his white flesh. Cassi imagined she looked the same way, but there was something that made the shadows dance with the light on his face. His features were accented under the streetlamp and softened, almost hidden, when he stepped out of the light. The stars burned around them, and the couple felt captivated by the darkness. Cassi felt her hand grow warm in his, their fingers laced. When she looked down at them she noticed the light on her fingers, and the shadows hugging his. The way light and dark played off him intrigued her, almost liquid, moving, as if it were alive.

They crossed under the lights of streetlamp after streetlamp, never ending light and dark. The stars flickered, enveloped them in fire, while the darkness engrossed them with a coolness that made the morning air wonderful. The mountain peaks began to glow a soft pink. When Cassi looked up, the school towered above her. Time had passed so quickly, and the horizon was lightly glowing.

Lucas pulled open the door, inviting her inside. She entered and turned to see the glass doors close behind him just as the sun burst over the mountain peaks. Light brought life to the world, and death to the shadows. Cassi peered at it, pondering. "I don't think I've ever actually taken the time to watch the sun rise, to enjoy it for what it is. It's always been just a ball of burning gasses to me, nothing more."

"You should see it set," Lucas responded, his eyes sparkling while the rest of him was hidden in the shadows of a classroom doorway.

The day moved slowly; time becoming a lazy river with no place to go. Cassi ambled slowly to her classes, not interested in what was going on. She didn't care about anything but sitting and getting lost in her own thoughts. Lunch came and went. As usual, Cassi ate outside with Rick. Lucas was nowhere in sight. This disappointed Cassi. She would have liked to introduce her two friends—or were they more than that to her?—she was afraid to think about it. She didn't want any feelings more than friendship. Why should she have to get involved with anyone? She was a whole person and didn't need anyone in her life to push *her* around. But every time Lucas came into her mind, she knew he wouldn't try to change her. He just wanted to help her realize her potential and encourage her to become who she really was.

The bell rang; the day finished. She met Lucas at the same door they had entered that morning. His smile brought warmth, and his eyes read all her secrets.

"Gotta stay after," he said with a quiet tone and a shrug. He looked at the floor with real disappointment showing on his face.

"That's okay, I'll walk her home," a voice echoed from behind Lucas.

He jumped and whirled around, catching sight of Rick. A hint of fear crossed his face, and he refused to meet Rick's eyes. Anyone looking at Lucas would notice the hatred fevering his features, but Rick remained calm, and Cassi couldn't take her eyes off him, as if some mystical force held them there. Rick glanced at Lucas, took Cassi kindly but firmly by the arm, and walked her outside into the sunlight.

"I don't like him," Rick stated when the building was out of sight.

Cassi stared, incredulous. "You don't even know him! Look what he's done for me!" she exclaimed, becoming defensive.

Rick's eyes calmed her quickly. "You're beautiful. You always have been. You don't need new clothes or a fancy hairstyle to tell you that."

Cassi replied, "For the first time, I feel like I am important, like I matter. He makes me feel so different, so unique."

"You are unique! But he is *different*."

"You make it sound like that's a bad thing."

"It's a bad kind of different."

"You don't know him like I do."

"I know him better then you think."

"If you would just give him a chance! Talk to him tomorrow at my birthday party. He'll be there."

Rick's eyes became apologetic. "I won't be," he stated quietly. "Tomorrow is also Good Friday. I know this doesn't make much sense, but I'm expected to be somewhere else. I guess you could call it an appointment that I can't miss."

Cassi looked hurt, but softened under his gaze.

"I'm truly sorry. You'll have fun anyway," he continued.

Cassi smiled. "That's okay. Just promise that you'll make it up to me sometime."

Rick laughed, "That I will, ten times over and more, especially if you aren't careful."

"Careful? Careful about what?"

Rick looked stuck between frustration and depression. "Just be careful," he said.

CHAPTER EIGHT

The sun fell. Lucas welcomed its colorful farewell salute as blessed freedom from its painful rays for a few sweet hours. The shadows crept from their hiding places and engulfed the world in their beauty. Lucas burst through the school doors, the cool air running over his body like the waves of an ocean. He was hungry. He walked the streets for what seemed like hours, heading gradually toward the outskirts of town, where, away from city lights, he could experience the blackness that he craved. No street lamps brightened the paths of those who would be out in this area at night.

He crouched. Someone was walking down the street, alone. Lucas glanced about him; no one else was in sight. His excitement grew. He loved this part, and the scenery was perfect: a gloomy alley that turned off a deserted street and a dark stranger making his way toward him. This stranger approached Lucas's hiding place, got closer, and passed. Lucas stood and followed like a shadow: quietly, swiftly. With a sudden leap he grabbed the victim and disappeared into the neighboring alley. The person struggled and tried to scream. Lucas could tell it was a teenager, a male, no more than nineteen-years-old. In the secluded alley, he tilted the struggling teen's neck, easily restraining him with his superhuman strength. Fangs appeared on Lucas's top jaw, his face turned twisted and monstrous. He leaned in closer and pierced the warm flesh. The bittersweet warmth filled his mouth. Lucas enjoyed it.

In this moment of pure ecstasy, the man was ripped from him—vanished. Lucas was dazed. When his focus returned, a young woman stood before him.

"Lucas?" the voice came in surprise.

Lucas smiled, a stream of blood dripping from his fangs and down his chin. "Dominique," he stated slowly. "He was already dead. You really should have let me finish my meal."

She didn't waste any time; after all, he wasn't just a schoolmate anymore. He was a vampire. She swung, feeling the successful connection of her fist on his face. She followed with another to the other side. Lucas was stunned, but shook it off. Then Dominique heard a low growl. It was too late—Dominique had already begun the third swing when Lucas grabbed her arm and swung her light body into the brick building that defined the alley. Dominique felt the vibrations from the blow echo through her bones. Pain shot up her arm accompanied by an unnerving crack.

"Now you've made me mad," Dominique

whispered fiercely, taking out a wooden stake she had tucked in her belt.

Even with Lucas still gripping Dominique's dangling arm, she had no trouble flipping him over her body. He landed with a loud thud and blacked out for an instant as the wind was knocked out of him. Dominique took advantage of that moment, and lunged. Lucas caught the stake as it pierced the flesh of his chest, but didn't enter far enough to damage his heart. They struggled momentarily against the other's strength, rolling. Dominique felt her body run again into the building. Lucas swung and connected with the side of Dominique's head, causing a rumbling in her skull as blood appeared in her ear. He stood and picked her up by her throat, holding her in midair. "Don't mess with the Prince of Darkness," he rasped and threw her into the wall again. She stayed on the ground in a crumpled heap, the pain surprisingly searing even to a slayer. Lucas turned and disappeared into the darkness.

"Nobody turns their back on me!" Dominique cried, knowing she was out of stakes. With one last-ditch effort she pulled a short, but razor-sharp, knife from her boot, angry with herself for not getting another stake instead. She spun the handle in her hand and threw it with all her remaining strength.

She heard it rip through Lucas's flesh with a slashing thud, followed by a low growl.

Lucas barked, "I should kill you for that!"

He spun around. Dominique could see his bright blue eyes, electric in the darkness. He raised his hands, and the alleyway filled with a dense fog.

Dominique stood. She was directly below an overhead light, a light that now was muffled by the thickening atmosphere. She could hardly breathe. She felt her feet leave the ground as she was grabbed from behind.

She instinctively struggled.

Then there was a rough whisper in her ear, "If you can't see it, it isn't really there, right? Perhaps I'll take just a taste."

Dominique gritted her teeth when she felt two cold fangs on her neck. "You wouldn't beat me in a real fight," she chortled. "Go ahead, hide in your fog, sneak up on me... you're not a prince; you're not even a man."

Lucas struck. Dominique cried in pain, but then he turned her toward him. She could see his face through the fog, completely disgusting. His fangs were still exposed, dripping with her blood.

"Remember what that feels like, slayer," he said, licking the blood off his fangs with a euphoric sigh. "I want you to remember that, so when I kill you, the last thought in your mind will be how it feels exactly like this night! For now, you are lucky. It is not your time. I'm going to let you live."

He thrust her into the wall with such force that she thought she heard her skull crack.

"Remember." He walked away calmly and called over his shoulder, "Remember how much you hate me."

Dominique struggled to stay conscious, but the pain in her throbbing head was too great. Her world slipped into darkness, but it soon became clear, as the fog around her followed its master into the night.

***

A lilting chime coursed its way through Cynthia's dimly lit house. Its beautiful bells rang twelve times before it fell silent. Dominique sat on the couch in the front room, cradling her broken arm. The Protector sat diagonally across from her in his usual chair.

"I've never had a vamp break a bone... I've never had a broken bone," Dominique whimpered, staring blankly ahead. "And he made off with my knife."

"He bit you too, it appears," Rick stated. "I stopped the bleeding. Lucas is very powerful; it is about time someone humbled you."

"I lost."

"Does that surprise you?"

"I came here to win, and I know you did too."

The grin on his face dwindled, "You can't win with a broken arm, now, can you?"

"*We* can't win with a broken arm," Dominique corrected.

"I suppose not. Now, if I use my power to heal you, you'll probably see your vision again. Are you ready for that?"

"If you show me the ending. I'd really like to know what happens."

He gave her an exasperated look.

"Oh come on... I know, I know," she responded. "Fate."

He stood, majestic power rising within him. The

house grew brighter. With every step he took closer to her, the pain in her arm subsided. The light from the overhead fixture streamed to his fingertips. When he stood in front of her, he reached down and lightly brushed her arm. For an instant Dominique couldn't breathe. She felt two-dimensional. She was falling head over heels, over again, three times. A white light flashed. It was violent, vibrant, and it was over.

It was always the same. She sat at a long wooden table with people who were very powerful. She could feel their power as though she were one of them. She wore a flowing white dress, and she felt the weight of a tiara resting on her head. She turned her gaze to her left and found herself sitting at the right hand of a man dressed in royal robes. He was laughing at a joke that she didn't hear. He raised a glass to his lips and took a large swig of ale. She could smell alcohol in the air around her. It was sickening. She knew who he was: he was Osiris, the god of Egypt—her husband. She realized she had also had a little too much to drink.

Then came trouble…

***

Dominique's eyes burst open as she gasped.

Rick was back in his chair, and she was back in her place on the couch, but her arm was unbroken, and the clock was chiming again.

"One o'clock?" Dominique asked sluggishly.

"Recovery was forty-seven of your minutes. If you meet Lucas again, stay away—it is not your responsibility to kill him."

"I'm a slayer," Dominique said, testing her arm by swinging it into a pillow. "If it isn't my job, whose is it?"

"He will decide."

Dominique paused and studied him curiously.

"I need to leave. It seems that the Powers That Be are expecting me."

"What is this Good Friday meeting about anyway?"

"Judgment Day."

"For whom?" she asked, but he was already gone.

***

Lazily moving clouds partially hid Friday's afternoon sun. The temperature was cool, and a soft breeze blew gently. Cassi sat on her porch steps, the wind whisking her loose hair across her face. She was content with life, excited, but something wasn't right, and she could feel it in the back of her mind, always there—persistent. This nagging feeling never revealed anything to her; it was simply there. Cassi decided she would worry about it after her birthday party tonight, but something told her that by then, it may be too late.

***

Cynthia, Dominique, and James sat quietly on the carpet in Cynthia's hallway with playing cards in their hands. Cynthia looked at the jacks, queens, and threes staring back at her. She collapsed them in her hands and threw them on the floor.

"Something doesn't feel right," she stated.

"Evil," Dominique responded.

"The balance of good and evil shifts without the Protector here," James said.

"The air feels heavy," Cynthia responded.

James met her eyes. "We have a lot to do—it's our burdens that are heavy."

Cynthia picked up her cards, only to set them down again with the words, "Two pair."

***

Lucas stared at his father; Set peered back at his son. Both grinned ever so slightly. The darkness encompassed them.

"I feel the path of this world is about to change course, Lucas," Set stated. "Soon we will rule here—completely, I mean."

Both breathed the stale air deeply and let it out with a euphonic sigh.

"You will finally get your revenge on Horus, it seems."

Set nodded, "Yes, perhaps I'll take from him what he took from me."

"Ah, your nephew and my half brother. I must have been conceived before your little... accident. I'd imagine living without... well... as you do, must be difficult. I still don't quite understand how you stole his mother from him, but I bet I know why she left!" Lucas retorted.

"I was beautiful once too, quite desirable. If it

hadn't been for his mother, you wouldn't be here. Oh, and *I* left when I chose to take over the underground… and took you with me."

"Well then, what are your plans for revenge against Horus?"

"Take another he cares about. I took his mother; you'll take his friend. Your job is to make her love you. Regarding which, do you feel ready for your wedding night now?" Set laughed. "Or do you still feel it a burden you are unwilling to bear?"

Lucas grinned. "Jealous, Father? Perhaps it is because I can still have offspring!"

"As can I. I just have a different type of offspring. Your offspring will be mine just as all the vampires are mine."

"Do you ever tire of this existence, Father?" Lucas asked.

Set paused. "Yes, my son. After thousands of years I am ready to turn my life over to a younger evil… if you think you are sufficiently prepared to reign."

"Are you ready to leave me?"

"Leave you? You were prophesied before this world began. You think I'll ever leave you? Someone needs to make sure you are doing things right!" Set joked. They both laughed. "I'm in the mood for a snack, want one?"

"No," Lucas responded.

His father stood from his stone throne in the wall and reached into a deep crevice, revealing a tiny kitten. "Pity."

"I need my bride first… before I can reign."

"Ah, so you are seeing the bigger picture, then?

Good. Just don't fall in love."

Lucas snorted. "Love. Pah! Where is the necklace for me to give to Cassi?" Lucas asked.

"Don't worry, Son." Set glanced at Lucas. "It will be at the party tonight."

"And you really believe its beauty will be enough to convince her to become one of us?"

"I believe," Set chortled, "she will be quite enchanted!"

CHAPTER NINE

The rain cleared just in time for Cassi's party. The sun dyed the tops of the snow-covered mountains a brilliant orange as it slid past them. A soft, warm breeze rustled through the trees, compelling the stale air of the early afternoon to become fresh again.

The first guest to arrive was Debbie, one of Cassi's closest friends. She parked her car next to the curb as the first stars were appearing. She walked up the sidewalk and handed Cassi a small, wrapped present.

"Happy birthday," Debbie said with a hug and a smile.

"Thank you," Cassi responded. "I'm glad to see you were able to make it. We were starting to get a little worried when you missed so much school. You were with your grandpa, right?"

Debbie forced a worried look off her face, only to realize it was okay for it to be there. "Oh that, yeah. Sorry I didn't call. I've been a bit distracted."

"I'm just glad you could make it."

Other friends began to appear, and by their numbers, it was easy to tell that Cassi was well liked by many, even if they weren't from the "popular" crowd. Even James, with his large, brown eyes and stern appearance, showed up, though he detested social occasions. As usual, he wore the pentagram necklace that he seldom removed.

James helped Cassi light candles that permeated the house with various fragrances. Their flames danced on the wick to the beat of the music that echoed from the living room. Cassi watched as James picked up the flame in his fingers and moved it from forefinger to thumb, letting it flicker on his flesh. The fire flowed over his hand before he finally replaced it on the wick.

Cassi laughed, "You're going to have to teach me that one!" she exclaimed with delight.

"I didn't think you had an interest in witchcraft," he responded, smiling.

"I was always taught that witchcraft was evil."

"Any power in the hands of the wrong person can be evil, but that same power in the hands of the right person can be good," he countered.

"I suppose so," Cassi replied.

James noticed her face fall pensive. The look bothered him. They were in a hallway that led from the living room to the upstairs bedrooms. The lights from both ends of the hall flooded the otherwise unlit hallway, allowing the glow from the candles to light Cassi's face ominously. "What is it?" he asked.

"Where have you been?" Cassi responded, not accusingly. "I haven't seen you around much."

"I know," James said. "I really don't know what is going on. I've been so… preoccupied. Changing schools has been challenging. The work isn't hard. I just think I'm going to be treated the same way wherever I go. The Wicca thing is taking a lot of time too. See, there's this thing… something in the air, I guess you could say. It isn't good. I've been busy trying to figure out what is going on, what could be coming. I'm worried about you."

"Me?"

"Well, yes. And everyone else I suppose. Whatever this is, it's powerful."

Cassi smiled. "See, if you weren't so heavy into this witchcraft thing you would have a lot less to worry about! Besides, seems to me that all this trying to protect me and everyone else is taking time from what is really important."

"Like what?"

"Our friendship," she responded. "I miss seeing you around, that's all. I don't have many close friends. You mean a lot to me."

James grinned, "I think you have more friends than it seems. I know things," he said, pointing to his head, "and even the gods are protecting you."

Cassi laughed, "Yeah, right. Did you cast a protection spell on me?"

James's smile widened, "Maybe."

A shout came from Debbie in the living room, "Hey Cassi, James, what are you two doing there in the dark hallway? You're supposed to be lighting *candles*. Let's get this party started!"

Soon the party activity turned to talking, food, and games. It was amid their laughter and conversation that a soft knock came at the door. It was barely audible, but it resonated inside Cassi's head as though it was destined for her. She could feel that tonight's events were inevitable and that knock was the beginning of what was to come.

Cassi walked down the stairs in a daze. She reached out and grasped the doorknob, the coldness biting into her hand. She hesitated before opening the door, and the sense of ominous foreboding sharply returned. She ignored the feeling, and pulled open the door to reveal Lucas, who stood waiting. He wasn't smiling, but she could feel a distant heat radiating from his soul; he cared so much about her. She smiled and invited him in. He took her hand immediately, and with Cassi in the lead, they walked up the stairs.

"Sorry I'm late," he shouted over the music. "I had the hardest time getting out of my house. I don't even think I left until sundown."

When they reached the top of the stairs, Lucas's focus changed. In the circle on the floor sat a strikingly familiar face. Her brown hair fell easily about her, but a look of horror immediately came over her when her round eyes caught sight of him. She refused to acknowledge him, her eyes seeking refuge in the carpet.

Lucas whispered in Cassi's ear, "Who is that girl?"

"Which one?" Cassi asked, unsure.

"The one sitting there…" Lucas motioned with his eyes, "the one staring at the floor."

Cassi hesitated. The music almost drowned out her

answer, but Lucas heard, "Debbie."

"Debbie," he repeated, loud enough that she looked up at him, her eyes wide and fearful.

Cassi looked bewildered.

"Can I talk to her for a moment?" Lucas asked, seeming agitated.

Cassi's bewilderment persisted, but for lack of a better answer, she responded, "Sure."

Lucas motioned to the girl who was trying so hard to avoid his gaze; she rose, even though she didn't see his hand motion to her, and followed him outside into the night air.

The moment the door sealed them outside, Debbie burst into tears. "Why are you following me? I'll do what was asked of me," she said between quick breaths.

He glared at her, confused. "You're the girl from the cavern, aren't you?" That night was clear in his mind; he had returned to his father's cavern, and the necklace had just been finished. A celebration was taking place, and his father presented a sweet girl a girl to him. This was that girl, but how was she still alive?

Debbie paused, looking angry. "You know what you are making me do!"

"No, I don't," Lucas said. "What are you talking about? Tell me what's going on!"

She almost softened, but then stood firm, "Don't play mind games with me."

"I thought you were dead," Lucas whispered, shaking his head, his mind becoming blurred.

"Dead?" The look she gave him next caused a new emotion to rise within him: fear.

He covered his eyes in frustration. "Tell Cassi I'll be back as soon as I can. Do not do *anything* until I return. I *do not* know what was asked of you, but do not do it! Do not do *anything*!" He turned his back on Debbie, took a deep breath, and ran into the night.

Debbie watched as the shadows covered him, racing after him to engulf him in their strong grasp until he vanished completely.

Debbie was confused, but went back inside, wiping the tears from her eyes. When she returned to the party, she had a smile on her face.

James smiled back at her. "Well, now that you're back, let's open presents!"

Cassi smiled in agreement.

"Shouldn't we wait for Lucas to come back?" Debbie asked.

"Come back? Where did he go?" Cassi questioned in response.

"He said he would be back soon."

"I don't think we should wait," James interrupted, opening his bag and pulling out a box.

Cassi took it from his outstretched hand and began unwrapping it slowly, peeling each piece of tape from the paper.

"Oh, just rip it," James laughed.

Cassi laughed, tearing the paper until she finally revealed what was inside. "*Buffy the Vampire Slayer*," she said.

"The boxed set," James continued.

Cassi looked at him with a grin. "My favorite show."

***

"Father!" Lucas cried, his voice echoing through the pitch-black cavern. The pillars of fire that normally provided light rekindled, burning eagerly in the stale air.

Set dropped from his resting place on the ceiling, landing lightly on his feet in front of his son.

"You sound agitated," Set spoke in almost a whisper. "You shouldn't wake me when you're agitated."

Lucas glared at him, fury emanating from his body. His eyes, which usually instilled trust, now contained hate. His emotions choked his speech. "What do you have planned?"

"For whom?"

"Me, Cassi, how about that girl… Debbie. Take your pick."

"I'm not sure I understand what you mean," Set stated calmly, obviously lying.

"Let me refresh your memory. The night the necklace was finished, a girl was presented to me at the celebration—"

"And you chose not to eat. I remember, Lucas."

"Why is she still alive?"

Set froze, "She has become one of my, eh, favorite mortals."

"Why?" Lucas barked.

"Well," Set chuckled, "I thought she would be one of yours too. After all, she is going to bring your bride to you tonight."

Lucas was confused, "What? Tonight is *our* night. I will be the one to change her. Debbie isn't even one of us. Father, have you forgotten, in your old age, that you must *be* a vampire to make a vampire? How is Debbie supposed to accomplish that?"

"One of my many minions will be at the place, waiting to change Cassi."

Lucas's eyes narrowed into slits, "What place? You've arranged her awakening without consulting me? What makes you think she will choose to become like you?"

"Not like me, like you," Set reminded.

"No. This is *not* how it will happen! I'm going back to the party. A complete stranger will not force this upon her. I will change her, by her choice, when the time is right," Lucas turned and started to walk toward the open world.

"Melanie!" Set commanded.

The first witch in Set's clan stepped into Lucas's path, blocking the only way out. Lucas hesitated in front of her before he growled, "Move."

"Never," Melanie hissed, meeting his glare.

"Then I will move you," he said and grabbed her shoulders.

Melanie held out her palm and sent Lucas flying through the air with a snapping burst of power.

He lay there on the ground, paralyzed. The room went silent around him. "Why?" he uttered.

"To ensure she succumbs."

"Without the choice, Horus will change her back," Lucas coughed.

"No, Lucas. Not with the necklace."

The necklace. His mind betrayed him; he was too

stunned to think. "What is the *real* purpose of the necklace, Father?"

Set kneeled over his son, his face soft, "To rescue the person who dons it from the blinding light of good."

"You are going to trick her into becoming one of us," Lucas stated.

"This girl is too important to us. We cannot risk losing her."

"Let me go to her," Lucas begged.

"I think you are too involved, Lucas. This is nothing but a charade to you, remember? No. You will not go to her. Tonight, my son, she will come to you."

***

Cassi laughed. "A pooping pig keychain? That's sick."

"Well," James said, "I guess that leaves just one more gift—Debbie's!"

"Wonderful! It's sitting on the coffee table. Could someone hand it to me please?"

The guests passed the small box around until it finally reached Cassi. She pulled off the bow, watching as the light it reflected refracted into millions of small rainbows that danced on the carpet. She peeled back the paper, revealing black velvet. She looked at Debbie and smiled, pulling the hinged lid open.

"Oh, Debbie," Cassi whispered, in awe over the simple beauty of the necklace. "Help me put it on."

The stones danced in James's eyes. A wave of

emotion flooded his mind. He attempted to shake it off, but the power of those stones overwhelmed him. He couldn't breathe, couldn't think. His vision was cloudy and the sounds of the room became muffled as if he were under water. A groggy sleep weighed his eyelids, blurring his vision.

"James. James!" Cassi shook his shoulders.

He looked at her, wearing the necklace that seemed to call to him.

"I've... must go," he choked out somehow. He tried to stand, but immediately lost his balance and fell down onto the floor with a painful thud. All he could think about was getting away, out. He stood again, forcing himself to focus on his balance, one foot in front of the other, down the stairs, and out the door into the night.

The other guests were bewildered.

"He'll be okay. He's James," Debbie stated after a long silence. "Come on, I have one more gift for you." She then said to the other guests, "We'll be back soon."

Cassi looked confused, "We're going somewhere?"

"We'll be back soon," Debbie repeated, sounding almost nervous.

"Shouldn't we wait for Lucas to come back?"

"How do you know he isn't part of the surprise?"

Cassi felt her heart leap. "You two have been planning something? Is that why he wanted to talk to you?"

"Something like that, yeah."

"But I just can't leave my own party," Cassi stated, glancing around at the other guests. Everyone was smiling at her.

"If Debbie's been planning something for your birthday, I think you should go," a voice resounded from the group, followed by general agreement. "You won't keep her long, will you, Debbie?"

"Of course not!" she said, and then turning to Cassi continued, "I'm sure it won't take very long. Let's just go have fun."

Cassi smiled, "You and Luke are really planning something?"

"And he promises it will be a birthday to remember."

"Then let's go!" Cassi clamored down the stairs, now excited. *I wonder where she's taking me,* she thought, climbing into the passenger seat of Debbie's car.

The car ride seemed to take forever because Cassi kept looking at the clock. The silence in the car indicated that Debbie was preoccupied, but Cassi was glad to have some time to think. She had missed Debbie lately. It was almost like something was wrong with her; she had become so reclusive. Even though they didn't say anything to each other now, Cassi was glad to be spending her birthday with her friend.

Finally, they pulled into a park where the pine trees surrounded a large grassy clearing. The stars above twinkled gracefully on their black stage, and the city lights reflected off the scattered clouds that drifted above, providing just enough light to see by.

Cassi stepped out of the car. "It's beautiful out here."

Debbie laughed nervously.

They walked to the center of the clearing before Cassi laid down, feeling the coolness of the grass seeping through her shirt. She stared at the stars. "I remember when we used to come here as kids."

"We had so much fun," Debbie recollected.

"Yeah," Cassi closed her eyes, a smile of contentment on her face. "Do you remember that time we ran away here to have a picnic lunch, just the two of us?"

"Yup," Debbie replied. "Little did we know that our parents planned it that way and followed us, watching us to make sure we were safe."

"I still got in trouble," Cassi chuckled. "I still remember my mom saying, 'If you ever run away for real I'm gonna—'"

Her sentence was cut short by a low rumble. Cassi sat up. The ground around her shook, twisted, and pulled. Pillars of fire leapt from the ground, three of them in a triangle with Cassi in the middle. Cassi looked at Debbie in fear. Debbie's eyes were downcast, and Cassi saw her mouth move in a whispered, "I'm sorry."

Cassi thought about running, but no human emotion was powerful enough to cause her concrete feet to move. She felt she was sinking into the soft soil as it came up to immobilize her.

"What are you sorry for?" Cassi screamed.

Everything went dark. The shadows in the park became more prominent. It fell silent. The hissing from the pillars of fire grew louder and louder until it exceeded the rumbling of a jet plane. Then it ended, and during the absolute silence, three figures stepped from the surrounding trees and took Debbie by the arms. "Excellent work, you did just fine. Your work is done; it's now your friend's time," they whispered.

Cassi was confused, but knew something was horribly wrong. "Debbie?" she questioned, but Debbie continued to stare at the ground.

Now another figure appeared, this one taller, leaner. Cassi could see the black figure coming toward her, its silhouette augmented by the light the flames cast. He paused to turn his face to the light. It was monstrous! Unnatural eyes glowed animal-like in the dim light. It had teeth, fangs. Cassi had only seen something like this on television shows and movies.

Cassi tried to escape, bolting toward the perimeter of the triangle she was held in. Yet, wherever she moved, the fire expanded to block her path. It was so hot that even from several feet away, the flames singed her flesh.

The beast entered the triangle and smiled. Cassi ran, determined to break through the flames, deciding that disfigurement from burning was better than what he might do to her. Then, she was falling. When she hit the ground her breath escaped her. Sharp pain raced up her leg from her ankle; the beast had hold of her. Cassi tried to scream but was immediately muffled by his hand clutching her mouth. She struggled, but he was too strong. His face appeared above her; closer it came until she could feel his hot breath on her cheek. She felt his lips brush her neck, like a touch of ice. Suddenly she felt excruciating pain, as though two sharp icicles had pierced her neck. She felt weak and could no longer struggle. At her greatest moment of desperation, when she was about to abandon herself to the shadows, the creature stopped. He pressed his wrist against her teeth and spoke for the first time, "I have control of your friends. Debbie is here," he said. With a snap of his fingers the three women brought Debbie into Cassi's view. "I also have Rick and Lucas. I'm sure not having them there spoiled your party… isn't that a pity. I'm going to kill them, but you can save them all. Drink from my wrist. That is all it takes. Just bite and your friends live. If you do not choose quickly, you will die, and so will they. Don't be selfish."

Cassi looked at Debbie, who was sobbing. "I don't care about me, let them go. What are you?"

"All you have to do to free them is drink. If you don't, I will kill Debbie now. Then, I will torture the only other friends you have in the world. I assure you that their deaths will be *very* painful. End this madness now."

Cassi paused for a moment longer. She couldn't bear the thought of Rick, of Lucas, going through something like this, so she closed her teeth around the flesh of his arm. He let out a brief moan. The rusted taste of stale blood coursed into her mouth. With the first swallow she twisted in pain; by the second, her heart began to fail. Her life passed before her: her family, her friends, the sadness and the happiness. She saved her friends, which was all that mattered to her. She was filled with incredible knowledge, the light, the dark; it all made perfect sense to her now. Debbie did this to her on purpose; she loved Debbie for that. Rick wasn't who he said he was, and she hated him now.

"Your work is done, and we have won," Sara, the second witch, said to Debbie. "Allow us to bestow upon you a gift, to show Set's appreciation."

She pulled out a beautiful round silver ball that immediately captured Debbie's heart. Even amidst the horror she was witnessing around her, this little silver ball stole her mind. She could think of nothing else but its exquisite beauty. It was small, and it pulled in the glow from the pillars of fire in a way that manipulated the light gradually into the darkness's shadows. Its luster reflected in Debbie's eye as Sara cast it at her feet. Smoke began to billow and surrounded Debbie, encasing her in a sea of darkness. She was puzzled at first, but as the smoke burst into flames, she understood. Her skin melted from her bones, and Debbie cried out in pain as the flames devoured her flesh.

Thunder sounded and lightning struck a nearby tree, shattering its bark into tiny shards of wood that flew through the air, piercing the night with staples of death. The witches walked over to Cassi and put their bony hands on the assailing vampire's shoulder in a form of congratulation for a job well done. Cassi was still drinking from his naked wrist.

Another bolt of lightning struck the ground, and the Protector stood where it hit. His eyes blazed with the fury of the world, and his book boasted of its power. He was dressed all in gold. His hair glowed white with energy.

The witches cried out to the vampire, "Do not let

her go; that necklace is the only thing that may save us!"

"This moaning evil I remove. Cast into the darkness! Fall! The moaning evil that is here befallen." A flick of the Protector's hand sent out a trickle of light that swirled through the air. The light came quickly and struck a barrier of darkness an instant before it would have destroyed all evil. It was dispersed as darkness normally yields to light, but now it was the darkness that remained.

"The necklace protects. Its purpose fulfilled!" the witches chanted triumphantly. "Praise Set and his powers of darkness."

The Protector looked stunned and vanished. Cassi saw the bolt of light that signaled his departure, hating him, hating light. The flow of blood from the beast's wrist ran dry as he burst into dust. One of the witches had killed him. Cassi saw her holding a wooden stake in her hand just before she had the sensation of reliving her childhood. Her parents were there, holding her tightly against them like they used to when Cassi was small. Eighteen Christmases and birthdays flew by as she watched them, seeing herself grow older each time. She relived even this moment over again, in all of its horror, and all of its glory. Then, her eyes closed, and the world went black.

CHAPTER TEN

The night passed just as Set had planned it—his work was easy without the slayers on patrol. They weren't out tonight because the entire army of good was contained within the safe walls of Cynthia's home. James, Dominique, Cynthia, and Rick sat quietly, all of them angry and horrified.

Finally Rick spoke, "Why were none of you out on patrol tonight?"

The slayers dropped their heads. Dominique answered, "You were gone. I talked Cynthia into taking a night off. We're not perfect you know. Sometimes we need a break! We've been working so hard this week. I figured one night wouldn't matter."

"You should have known that Set would take advantage of my absence."

"I'm... sorry," Cynthia whispered, hanging her head in shame. "I feel awful."

"I know you do. As you should. I would expect such irresponsibility from Dominique, but you Cynthia?

You have always been the one I could count on, the one I could trust. You have sacrificed so much for Cassi already, and the one night, the one night she needed you to do your job, you failed her. Don't you all see? All the work we were doing was for *this* night. It all came down to this moment, and we failed!"

By this time, tears streamed down Cynthia's cheeks. She couldn't speak because her body was too tense from her uncontrollable sobs.

Dominique was furious. "How dare you? How can you blame this on us? Where were you during all of this?" she accused him defensively. "You disappeared; we had no idea when you would be back or where you were, and you expect us to save the world? Slaying is our job, saving *good* is yours!"

"I…" he paused, unsure of himself for perhaps the first time in his existence. "I was being… punished… by the Powers That Be… for interfering with fate." His voice rose in anger, "I brought you here without permission, Dominique, and in order to restore the balance of power, I was forced to watch as *my* best friend was fooled into betraying all that is good, into becoming a servant of my lifelong enemy. That is where I was: in hell. Do you know what hell is like? It is a place without agency. I had to experience that. I didn't have a choice. That is *my* excuse. *What is yours?*"

Dominique was silent. She didn't know how to answer. "Perhaps you should have thought about that before stealing Cassi's friendship away from Cynthia."

The Protector looked hurt. "You've crossed the line."

"Wait," James said in a calming voice, holding up his hand like a referee in a ballgame. "You just said she was fooled into becoming a vampire. Doesn't that justify you returning her soul? Since she didn't freely choose evil, if the choice was made forcefully for her, can't you do something? Not even evil can take away her agency without her choice. That would also be against fate's design, wouldn't it?"

"Hence the balance," the Protector said. "However, you are correct. Under normal circumstances I would have the ability to release Cassi's soul from Purgatory and return it to her body, but we have another problem. Remember that spell you were trying to figure out? It appears that Set has devised a talisman, a necklace that Cassi is wearing that keeps her from my powers of good, protecting anyone who dons the stones… Protecting… bah! More like entrapping…"

"Is that the necklace James saw at the party? The one he was telling us about that made him freak out?" Cynthia asked. Then turning to James, she said, "No offense."

"His response to the stones was consistent with such a forceful evil, I suppose."

"Then what are we supposed to do?" Dominique asked. "We can't kill her. Surely she'll be with Lucas twenty-four/seven, not to mention all the other demons that are surely willing to protect them. If she is some chosen one, and evil knows that, they aren't just going to let her wander around alone. It was bad enough trying to protect her when she wasn't a vampire, and now they have her? What *can* we do?"

"Get Cassi alone, fight her if necessary, and destroy the necklace," Rick stated.

"That isn't going to be as easy as it sounds," Cynthia said.

"No," Rick continued. "It will be virtually impossible unless the dark somehow yields to the light, but it's the only way. We must keep fighting and hope that evil will make a mistake. It is the power and strength of the night that will cause us problems, not the people it shelters."

"Night is an actual force? Scary!" Cynthia muttered.

"What about the legend?" Dominique asked, a sudden idea entering her mind. "It said that One could make light prevail. If you're that One, it should be easy, right? You just need to find out what you need to do to overpower the necklace."

The Protector remained silent.

"She's right," Cynthia said. "Who else would be able to make evil yield if not the One of light?"

"I agree," James added. "After all, you are the One *Amun-Ra* is written for. It makes sense that the legend's allusion to a powerful good would be you."

Dominique just stared into Rick's vacant eyes. "You don't know what to do, do you? You *are* the One that can make good win, right?"

Before Rick could answer, the doorbell chimed through the house, interrupting his thoughts.

Cynthia shook her head, squeezed her eyes shut as though she was just adjusting to the dim light, and walked toward the door. As she passed through the hallway, she knocked over a broom that had been leaning against the wall.

"Trouble is coming," Rick stated, without the slightest hint of surprise in his voice.

James looked at him seriously. "She knocked over a broom. Trouble is already here."

Cynthia pulled open the door, revealing a darkly dressed female police officer with a badge that caught the hallway light and reflected it back into Cynthia's eyes.

The woman introduced herself, "Hello, I'm Officer Allred. I need to speak with a Mister... hmm, Rick. I was told I would find him here."

Cynthia's eyes widened, questioning.

Rick was already at the door. "I am the person you seek."

Cynthia glanced at the two of them, worried about the look in their eyes. She turned and walked away, leaving them to talk privately.

The officer continued as soon as Cynthia was out of earshot, "I am here because of a very interesting call I received this evening. It seems that a girl you know is missing. The last time anyone saw her was in a park just south of here. A witness identified you at the scene. I need to ask you a few questions about her disappearance."

"A witness? Who?"

"Normally we don't answer that question, but since it was an anonymous call anyway..."

"Kendra..." Rick opened his mouth to speak, but instantly realized his mistake.

The officer stared at him. "How did you know my

name?"

Rick remained silent for a moment before speaking, "Let's just say we were meant to cross paths."

She was flustered, almost angry. "Have we met before?"

"No, but we will meet again."

Her anger grew. "You're probably right, and with riddles like that I'm *sure* we will. I'm not going to rest until I get to the bottom of this girl's disappearance. Would you tell me where you were earlier tonight?"

"Out of town on business. Everyone in this house could tell you that."

"A little young for a business trip, aren't we?"

"A little young for an officer of law, as well, it seems," Rick responded, noting that this officer looked like she too, was only in her upper teens.

Allred's eyes narrowed. "Did anyone see you on this business trip? Where exactly did you go? How was it that you were seen at the scene of the crime?"

"There was no crime," Rick stated. "You said so yourself; the girl is *missing*."

"Where was the business trip?" Allred prodded.

"Look, Cassi and I were friends, very good friends. So I don't know what you are implying, but you shouldn't worry yourself with things you don't understand, and Cassi is one of those things," Rick stated, sounding agitated himself.

"Mistake number two, Buddy," Allred stated. "How did you know the missing person's name? I never told you it was Cassi who was missing, and I'm sure you know more than one girl."

"You would be surprised at what I know."

"What does that mean?" Allred snapped.

"All my friends are contained in this house. Cassi is the only one that doesn't *live* here with us. So pardon me for knowing that all my other friends are safe."

"Did I call her your friend? I only said someone was missing, and that you were seen there. You tied it back to Cassi, not me. I think I need to take a look around your property."

"Do you have a warrant?" Rick asked, knowing perfectly well that she didn't.

Allred paused, "No. Do you have something to hide?"

"The universe has many secrets. I hold the key to all of them."

Allred's face twisted in a wicked smile. "I was hoping you would say something like that. I think we are done for now."

"For now," Rick repeated. "Until we meet again."

***

"Here is the book," three whispers emerged from the darkness. "Would you like to do the honors, Lucas?"

"Should I? I've never awoken anyone before."

"You are the Prince of Evil, and she your bride to be. Surely she would want you to waken her. Just read here."

Lucas began to read:

> The Osiris the scribe Ani, whose word is truth,

saith, "The place which is closed is opened; the place which is shut is sealed. That which lieth down in the closed place is opened by the Ba-soul which is in it. By the Eye of Horus she is delivered. Ornaments are established on the brow of Ra. My stride is made long. I lift up my two thighs in walking. I have journeyed over a long road. My limbs are in a flourishing condition. I am Horus, the Avenger of his Father, and I bring the Urrt Crown and set it on its standard. The road of souls is opened. My twin soul seeth the Great God in the Boat of Ra, on the day of souls. My soul is in the front thereof with the counter of the years. Come, the Eye of Horus hath delivered for you your soul; my ornaments are established on the brow of Ra. Light is on the faces of those who are in the members of Osiris. Ye shall not hold captive my soul. Ye shall not keep endurance my shadow. The way is open to my soul and to my shadow. It seeth the Great God in the shrine on the day of counting souls. It repeateth the words of Osiris. Those whose seats are invisible, who fetter the members of Osiris, who fetter Heart-souls and Spirit-souls, who set a seal upon the dead, and who would do evil to me, shall do no evil to me. Hasten on the way to me. Thy heart is with thee. My Heart-soul and my Spirit-soul are equipped; they guide thee. I sit down at the head of the great ones who are chiefs of their abodes. The wardens of the members of Osiris shall not hold thee captive, though they keep ward over souls and set a seal on the shadow which is dead.

Heaven shall not shut thee in."[*]

Her eyes were too heavy to open, but she could feel someone's hot breath on her body. She felt like she was coming out of a deep sleep and couldn't understand her drowsiness. It was difficult to move at first, but slowly she began to regain feeling in her cold fingers. Her sense of smell returned; a musty odor filled her nostrils. She bent her toes, only to feel someone slowly caress them. She smiled, warm. Her body filled with newfound energy. Her vision blurred as she forced her eyes to open and to focus on a familiar face.

"Lucas," Cassi choked out.

"How are you feeling?" he questioned.

"Fine," she answered, lying.

He smiled. "I'm glad. I was a little worried that you wouldn't be so happy with me when you woke up. I'm sorry I couldn't have been there to be the one to change you. I wanted to be so badly."

Cassi looked solemnly at him. "I would have never freely chosen to become like this."

"And now that you are like this... like me?"

Cassi gave him an apologetic glance. "I feel different. I don't know how to explain it. Happiness is gone, yet there is no sadness. I know things, hidden things. Completely hidden. They are hidden to the world, to the people within it; they were hidden from me, but no longer. I can't be upset or angry with you. It is what you are."

Lucas smiled. "It is incredible, isn't it? No good, no evil. You have so much power, so much potential. You are going to live forever in a life of worldly pleasures, satisfying your every whim with a simple whisper of darkness. Cassi, Cassi… if you don't love it now, you will soon, I promise."

"Why didn't you tell me what you were? Who you are?"

He looked down at the cavern floor. "I was afraid of what you would have thought of me, of our friendship, of our… love."

She looked at him. "I remember her, the person I used to be. You're right. I would have never loved you for telling me the truth. In fact, I would have hated you… if I had even believed you." She chuckled. "It feels like my past life was just a dream, a fleeting moment, and this is who I am, this is the person I am supposed to be."

Lucas kissed her cheek and whispered in her ear, "Wake up then, darling. Your life has begun."

She turned her head and caught his lips. Her eyes closed, and she saw the world dance in her head. She felt weak. Her body was numb. The kiss, that actually lasted only moments compared to the time she had waited for it, seemed to last forever. Perfect pleasure embraced her entire being, but there was a hole there— the pleasure wasn't embracing her soul.

The realization made her stop.

Lucas pulled back, almost looking offended. "What?" he asked.

Cassi shook the thoughts from her head. *It was this life that was the dream, this life that was unreal. She no longer had her soul; she had lost her identity.*

Lucas sensed her thoughts. "Don't worry, that happens from time to time when you first get changed. It will wear off eventually. Your mind hasn't given in to all the vampire has to offer yet, even though your body has. It creates confusion, I know. But soon your mind will catch up, and all will be fine. You will have a new passion for this existence, a romance for the unseen, and a taste for the forbidden. I can't wait to share it with you."

"No, there is something else," Cassi stated. "Something's missing. I'm not supposed to be *this* person. I am another. There is another purpose for my life."

"To be with me," Lucas said.

That took Cassi by surprise. "What?" she asked shocked, realizing now that she was standing. The comment sent cold shivers down her spine.

Lucas walked to her and took her shoulders firmly in his hands. His eyes burned with an intense fire that Cassi had never seen before. He concentrated on her eyes, watching the light from the pillars of fire dance clearly in the shaded portions. The shadows hugged her, but the light still prevailed in her eyes.

"Marry me," Lucas suddenly blurted out.

Cassi melted under his gaze, and she wanted too much to make her lips utter the word *yes*, but there was still that something, a lull nagging at the base of her skull, telling her she wasn't supposed to be there, to be with him, to be evil. She felt the coolness of the shadows around her and could hear them whisper the secrets of the world to her, whisper the answer she wanted to say to him. She remained frozen, unable to speak, unable to say yes, and not wanting to say no.

When she didn't answer, his head fell in disappointment. His eyes returned to meet hers. "I'm sorry. That was too soon. Just think about it. The question will always stand."

He brushed the necklace that still hung around Cassi's neck. She felt its cool gems resting softly against her moon-kissed skin.

Her thoughts regrouped, and her body began to give her an overwhelming sensation. It took her a moment of concentration to remember what that feeling was. Then she tore her eyes away from his and said, "I'm... hungry."

"I'm glad, because I brought you a meal," Lucas said, reaching around a dark corner and easily lifting a person from a crevice in the darkness, a boy that was so young, sixteen at the most, and terrified.

"No," Cassi stated sharply. "I can't kill!"

"Then I'll do it for you, and you will only have to drink," Lucas mumbled without feeling.

"No, not one so young!"

Lucas chuckled. "Youth makes the best meal. They are small, powerful, supple, and so full of lust. Their blood is warm, not stale with time. You'll enjoy him." He took the boy's head firmly in his hands and quickly twisted. Following a sudden snapping sound, the boy gasped and fell limp.

Cassi's eyes widened. "Why did you do that?"

Lucas remained calm and let the body fall from his arms. "I would never expect you to do it, kill him on

111

your first night as a vampire, so I took care of that part for you. Drink quickly, before his blood grows cold."

"I cannot."

Lucas paused, frustrated. "You will grow weak if you do not eat, so weak that with time your flesh will fall from its bones. Your lust for blood will continue to grow until it consumes you. There is no reason why you should not partake now."

"I cannot," Cassi repeated. "It is too... unnatural."

Lucas clenched his fists. "His blood gets colder every second. He is already dead; it is too late for him! Drink!"

"If you are so worried about the blood going to waste, you do it!"

Lucas considered. "Only under one condition," he said. "After I drink from him, you drink from me."

"Can we do that?"

"For now, like a mother weaning a small child. Eventually, my blood will not satisfy your thirst. Hopefully by then, you will be ready to kill for yourself."

Lucas bent over the limp body and submerged his teeth into the warm neck. He beckoned to Cassi, and she came. Instinct settled in, and she pierced Lucas's neck, knowing exactly what to do and how to do it. His blood was stale, the nutrients from it being almost depleted, but there was another blood mingling with his own, blood that was full of life's energy, full of passion. It was warm, and Cassi could feel her strength multiply ten times over. She had never felt this strong, this powerful. She felt a desire stir within her, and pulling harder, she drank more deeply. The sensation was incredible. She wanted more.

"Stop," Lucas cried.

Cassi heard the word echo like a dream in her mind, but she was so full of passion that its meaning was beyond her comprehension. She drew even harder against Lucas's neck.

"Stop!" Lucas cried again, with a push so powerful that Cassi flew off his body, slid across the floor, and slammed into the opposite cavern wall. For a moment, blood continued to flow from the piercing in Lucas's flesh; her teeth tore gashes in his neck when he threw her off, but in seconds, the blood vanished and he was healed. He crawled a moment on the floor, his strength lost to him. "You lack the discipline it takes to stop yourself before you drain someone."

Cassi licked the remaining blood off her lips and stood. "That was incredible. Do you always get this sense of power?"

Lucas smiled, finally gaining the strength to stand. "You always gain the power of the person. The sensation will never be that strong with a mortal, unless, of course, you drink from the slayers."

"I already want more."

"Would you be willing to kill for it?"

Cassi hesitated. "Yes."

"Then my blood had quite the effect on you."

"You knew it would. As I drank from you, I could hear your thoughts."

"I knew it would eventually, but this turnaround came much more quickly than I expected. You will become a great and extremely powerful vampire, with time."

"And then what?"

"Then, together, we will rule the world. Now let's go out. I need to renew my strength. Let me teach you some tricks on how to suck the life out of someone!"

CHAPTER ELEVEN

The night was cold, the moon dark. Even the stars seldom dared to flash their dim light upon the face of the world. Cynthia and Dominique walked briskly without much thought, but with careful observation of the black world around them.

"We should split apart here. I'll take the east side of town; you take the west," Dominique said.

"Oh, of course you get the rich side," Cynthia joked, trying to lighten the looming deeds ahead of them. "Have a good night!" she said, turning down a dark street.

Cynthia walked for a long time, but met no one. Her heart pumped harshly in her chest. With the increasing number of vampires walking the streets, her job had become more difficult. How could she concentrate not only on finding Cassi, but also on ensuring the safety of all the innocent people in her town of Pleasant Grove?

At that thought, Cynthia couldn't help but chuckle to herself. Out of all the possibilities, the town where all evil contained itself, where the vampires chose to congregate, was named Pleasant Grove.

The clouds were beginning to clear. Above her, Cynthia saw the stars finally boasting their beauty.

"I knew you couldn't stay away for long. You are so used to being admired," she spoke to them. Cynthia stared at them, finding the constellations that she remembered learning years ago: Orion, the Big Dipper, and a large W that she couldn't remember the name of. It seemed to be the brightest tonight, that W in the sky, as if it were more important than the others.

"Could you be any more proud?" Cynthia asked the stars, smiling, then laughing at the idea that the stars cared what people thought of them.

Her mind returned to the task to which she had been assigned: fighting to free this small town, and the world she imagined, from the bondage of evil. She allowed herself one last thought of the stars, of a dying dream, before the clouds returned the sky to darkness, and she was brought back to her life and the job before her.

Even though the weight of the wooden stakes tucked into her belt was minimal, Cynthia felt as though the world's weight rested on her shoulders. She didn't notice how far she had walked, but she was now in an alleyway that twisted between two apartment buildings on the far west side of town. Her heightened senses began to play tricks on her, her ears hearing sounds like the soft patter of cat paws on the pavement. Though her heart feared what could be in the alley, her mind refused to give in to the possibility that anything could hurt her. After all, she knew she was a slayer. She knew who she was.

Cynthia stepped onto a main street, emerging from the alley. An overhead streetlamp caused her shadow to stretch across the sidewalk, onto a patch of lawn, and finally to be cast across the blacktop; but she wasn't alone. Cynthia watched another shadow grow behind her own. The shadow reached her foot, consuming it in blackness. The person was close, but not yet close enough to cause Cynthia any worry. Yet, she carefully watched the darkness encroach upon her own shadow and spread onto the lawn. Whoever (or whatever) it was moved fast, coming up quickly on the small slayer. The streetlamps that lined the street suddenly sparked, then blackened with the sharp sound of breaking glass, and soon both shadows were engulfed by the all-encompassing darkness. Cynthia spun on one well-balanced heel and met a twisted face whose black eyes peered into her own.

She smiled and with complete nonchalance said, "Hi."

The face grinned, and the being performed a sharp bow. "I'm going to enjoy this, aren't I?"

"Not as much as I am," she stated, thrusting one fist sharply into his jaw. The connection felt good to Cynthia, and the vampire fell back with a painful thud. He regained his footing quickly, as Cynthia knew he would. She took out one wooden stake from her belt and prepared for the kill. The vampire did everything just as Cynthia expected; he came after her with animal ferocity, like a jaguar closing in on its prey. Cynthia enjoyed the fight. The fists of the adversaries flew. Cynthia blocked and followed with a quick right-left kick and uppercut. The vampire responded by dodging, blocking, and then flying through the air from the force of Cynthia's blow. He growled, and drops of sweat trickled down his brow. Cynthia smiled, poised, and invited him for another round with the motions of her hand. Then things went suddenly wrong. Cynthia felt her feet leave the ground, and a pair of unbreakable hands held her against a strong body. She struggled as the vampire she had been fighting smiled, while another held her captive.

"Now who's having fun?" the vampire questioned, forcing the stake out of Cynthia's hot hand, playing with the tip of it over his heart. His teeth were exposed in anger. "I'm going to make this hurt…"

Then a familiar voice shouted, "Hello, I'd like to introduce you to Mr. Wood!"

The hands that held Cynthia immediately slackened, and dust settled around her feet. Cynthia quickly pulled another stake from her belt and thrust it into the first assailant's heart, a smile of great felicity crossing her face.

"What would you have done without me?" Dominique asked, still behind her.

Cynthia turned to meet her with a smile. "You are supposed to be on the *east* side."

"Something told me that you were having more fun, and I was right. Good thing I showed up too. It looked like you were having a bit of trouble."

Cynthia focused her gaze on the ground. "It just seems like the vamps have been stronger lately. From the second you got here I've had nothin' but trouble! I used to be able to take ten with no problem, and now…"

"Ten, yeah right," Dominique said.

Cynthia chuckled, "You know what I mean."

Dominique put her hand on Cynthia's shoulder. "You know, I think you're right. I have no doubt that you can kick some serious vampire butt, but we all need help sometimes, right? Maybe we should consider patrolling together from now on."

Cynthia looked up and smiled. "I thought you hated it here."

"I do, but not because of the people… okay, because of *some* people. But our kind? We slayers need to stick together. Besides, it will be more fun."

Cynthia took Dominique's hand and pulled her in for a hug.

"Okay, if you ever hug me again, I'll just let you die the next time," Dominique said with a laugh.

"Then maybe I shouldn't tell you that there is a tall-dark-evil-personage-like figure behind you," Cynthia said and tossed a stake into Dominique's awaiting hand. Dominique spun with great force and pushed the wooden object into another vampire's heart.

"That make's three in one night. Time for some pizza?"

Cynthia snickered. "So, you named your stake, huh? Mr. Wood?"

Dominique shot her a killer glance. "That is not discussed outside the two of us."

"Well, I suppose it's better than Mr. Pointy."

***

Meanwhile, the east side of town was quiet. A warm breeze blew lazily from the south, drying the newly born leaves on the trees. To Cassi it felt like the very first breeze, she herself being newly born. Lucas held her from behind, his powerful arms protecting her as they hid together in the shadows.

"I have taught you all I can without showing you. Just pick someone."

"Will it hurt them?" Cassi asked.

"Did it hurt you?"

"I remember feeling cold. It only hurt when I drank from him."

"You don't have to kill them. Drink just a little; they'll actually find it enjoyable. Remember when I killed the young man so we could drink? My father was angry because I didn't give the boy the chance to accept our gift of immortality. If you don't give them the chance to change into one of us, that anger may be turned toward you as well, so pick someone you think may accept our gift."

"I've been thinking about that. I think I'll choose someone old, because the gift of immortality may appeal to them."

"It might not be as easy as that. The gift of immortality will appeal to anyone who is prideful, or afraid of death. It is more a kind of personality you must find, not an age group."

"Shhh," Cassi whispered. "Someone's coming."

They crouched deeper into the shadows. "It's all about instinct," Lucas reminded. "Instinct will lead you. Just be subtle about it."

Cassi stepped out onto the street.

"No, not yet!" Lucas reprimanded, but he was too late.

Cassi glanced behind her. No one was around but Lucas and this man.

"Well hey, little lady," the man stated as she confronted him. He was younger than she had wished, probably in his early forties, and there was a gleam in his eye, one Cassi didn't appreciate. "You're out a bit late; looking for someone?"

Cassi smirked, deciding to use the little glimmer in his eye to her advantage: "Maybe I'm looking for you."

The man's eyes brightened. "I was hoping you'd say that," he said.

Cassi knew his type and suddenly felt no remorse for what she was about to do. "Well, let's get this party started," she said provocatively, moving a little closer.

"How much do you charge?"

"For you, tonight… it's a one-time, free trial offer," she stated, as he moved in a little closer. *That's it, she thought, just one step closer. Keep coming. There. Now!*

With amazing strength, she grabbed his jacket and pushed him to the ground, allowing herself to topple on top of him.

"Geez, baby, right here?" he choked.

Cassi gave him a sinister smile. She pushed her hair out of her eyes and replied, "Right here."

Simultaneously she covered his mouth with her hand and submerged her fangs into the man's neck. Lucas was right; instinct was dictating to her exactly what she needed to do. She was a natural. The man screamed and struggled at the initial shock, but soon relaxed and began to enjoy the sensation of her forbidden kiss. As his heart began to slow, and feeling his fresh blood course through her tired veins, she stated in a powerful manner, "Now drink from me, or die."

"Wow," the man said dreamily, "anything for you," and he bit deeply into Cassi's bare wrist.

Cassi stood as his body turned cold and he no longer drank. "That feels *so* good," she licked her lips, turning to Lucas, who had emerged and was now only a few steps behind her.

He sniffed and nodded his head. "So much for subtlety."

"He's going to join us!" Cassi beamed.

"Uh huh," Lucas chortled, continuing to nod his head. "Well, Father would be pleased. On second thought," he walked to the body on the sidewalk and nudged it with the toe of his boot, "no, he isn't."

He pulled a stake from the depths of his leather jacket and thrust it into the man's heart.

Cassi looked at him, bewildered. "Why did you do that?"

Lucas grinned, took Cassi in his arms, and said, "You did well, a little forward for my taste, but quite good. I just don't like competition."

"Worried?" Cassi teased.

"Nah. I just didn't like the way he looked at you."

***

The sun rose, painting the sky the colors of a stained glass window. It rose over the mountaintops, burning with the fury of a marching army of light.

Lucas watched it coming. Through the crevices that marked the entrance to their underground cavern, he could stay in the shadows and watch it rise. He dodged the light beams that shot at him, playing it like a game, avoiding their burning arms by ducking into the shadows that ensured his safety.

Cassi snarled at him. "My first day as a vampire, and even I know to stay out of the sun."

His eyes sparkled as he jumped at her, tackling her to the ground. "You don't know everything."

Cassi laughed as his weight bore down on her. "I guess I know more than you... now get off me!"

She pushed, surprised at her own strength as she easily threw him off her body. He rolled, yawned, and laughed blissfully. "Once you live long enough, the sun becomes more of an annoyance than anything else. The darker you get, the more control you have over the light. I've been in the sun before. It weakens me greatly, even burns, but it can no longer kill me. I have the ability to control my desire to go toward the light. I think you'll learn quickly. In just a few centuries, you'll play games with the light too."

They laid there together, staring at the bats already in deep slumber hanging from the ceiling. The silence was welcome, not at all an awkward moment between them. Cassi liked that. She could remember very few awkward moments they had shared, even though there had been a few odd ones.

"Do you love me?" Lucas suddenly asked.

Cassi's eyes widened, somewhat surprised, but not stunned. He had turned this into one of those odd moments. Her mind became jumbled, her answer unclear. Yet, she knew what she wanted to say, and for once, her heart overpowered her mind.

"Yes."

"Then marry me."

This time it was her heart that became jumbled and her mind that cleared. Cassi was plunged into a dark place, unable to find any light. Her chest hurt; her body hurt. Unable to speak, she turned and saw Lucas still staring at the cavern ceiling, patiently awaiting her answer. He then realized that something must be wrong and turned to her, resting his head on one arm. "Collecting your thoughts?"

"I just... didn't expect that."

"What? I've asked you before, so you must have known it was coming."

"No, it isn't that... I just..."

Lucas kissed her elbow and gave her a look that demanded an answer.

"I'll have to think about it. Excuse me."

She stood and walked away, leaving him there on the cold, stone floor. He gave her a quizzical look from behind; Cassi could feel his gaze burning into her back. She turned and headed deeper into the cavern, plunging herself into a blacker darkness. Her eyes adjusted quickly, the animal instincts in her becoming more evident. She could feel them taking over. She pushed open a heavy wooden door and thrust herself past the three witches who happened to be on their way out to meet Lucas. They hissed as her shoulders collided with their frail bodies.

Cassi sat alone in the darkness and confinement of her room. She knew she wanted to marry Lucas. Her *instincts* told her she wanted to be his bride, but there was something deep within her that had been holding her back since the time she first succumbed to the evil within her. There was some good left that haunted and angered her, causing the *real* her to become silent and to cloud her thoughts if she tried to think like her, like the person she had become.

She stood and paced, again attempting to think of her life with him, her future as she was now. Again, her head became full of piercing light, blinding her thoughts and causing pain in her temples so intense that she let out an unearthly cry. Yet, when she thought of saying no, of being the person she was before, her mind instantly cleared and her thoughts grew cool and calm. In her confusion, she didn't realize that someone else had come into the room.

"I shouldn't have asked so soon. Your mind hasn't become like mine yet, but the longer you live like us, as us, the smaller that persistent nagging will become, until you squeeze it out of your mind like an annoying fly.

You will become like us. You will... become."

"That sounds great, Lucas," Cassi snapped. "But for now, will you please just leave me alone?"

He didn't say another word, just turned in the darkness and respected her request.

A silver tear slid down Cassi's cheek and fell lightly on her clenched hand. She flicked it off instantly, ignoring the coolness it brought to her already freezing skin. Her heart wasn't pumping; the blood within her was cold. How? How could she live like this, as if two people were in her head, pulling her skull apart?

CHAPTER TWELVE

"You have *feelings* for him?"

"No, not exactly. I just thought he was good looking, but then he goes for that Cassi chick," Dominique laughed. "I don't think I want a vampire as a boyfriend anyway. Sooner or later I'd have to kill him."

"Didn't you kill your last boyfriend anyway? He wasn't even a vampire," Cynthia said sarcastically.

"Good joke, ha ha, whatever. They call that a *freak accident*."

"Did he really die?" Cynthia asked, becoming instantly serious, afraid she'd hit a nerve.

"No!" Dominique cried, "of course not. I'm a slayer, remember? We don't have much time for a social life. But Luke, hmmm, I would have made time for him, had he not been a Cassi-lovin', blood-suckin' fiend!"

Cynthia snickered. "Hey! Cassi isn't that bad, once

you get to know her. Remember? She used to be my friend."

Dominique rolled her eyes. "She is such a... a... I can't even describe her."

"Well, just think of it like this: now if you meet her along the street, you can slay her!" Cynthia joked.

Dominique was amused. "Who decided she was the chosen one anyway? I don't remember seeing her in the prophecy I read."

"Well, why not read it again?" Cynthia suggested.

"I don't think the Protector would be amused if I asked him to read it again. He would take it as me doubting his authority."

Cynthia took a sip of her hot chocolate. "You don't have to ask him. He left *Amun-Ra* for James to study upstairs."

Dominique smiled mischievously and broke into a run for the stairs. Cynthia followed, almost choking on the hot liquid she poured down her throat. They flipped on lights as they went, excitedly fumbling the switch on in James's study.

There it glowed, sitting open on a small table.

"He would be so mad," Dominique said. "Where are James and Rick anyway?"

"I have no idea, something about buying something-or-another for some spell. James said not to worry about the book because it can't be taken from the room, some protection spell. So what's wrong with looking at it in the room?"

"Do you always ramble when you're nervous?" Dominique asked.

"Well, actually yes. There was this one time... I'll shut up."

Dominique laughed and then turned her attention to the gleaming book. "What page is it on?"

She turned a golden page, watching the light reflect oddly off its pages. *The prophecy*, Dominique thought. Her mind focused on the symbols on the pages, searching for any sign of familiarity. As if reading her thoughts, *Amun-Ra*'s pages began to turn themselves over, the light pulling like tiny strings causing the pages to float. It paused and fell open to a golden, shimmering page. This page's beauty defied all other. Flowing like water, its symbols changed with every breath that Dominique took. She focused her eyes like she would for a magic eye poster, and her mind fell into the page, passing words and Egyptian letters, attracting her like magnets attract metal. She was scattered in thousands of directions, until finally her mind fell upon a familiar text.

Dominique read it again, still uncertain of its meaning. After her third time through the passage, the sound of her name pulled her out of her trance.

"Dominique!"

She blinked and returned with a, "Huh?"

Rick and James stood in the doorway, their faces cross with anger and questioning. "What's going on here?" Rick demanded, his voice sounding both magnificent and immortal.

"Just trying to understand your prophecy," Dominique stated shyly, forgetting the whole truth.

Rick crossed his hands behind his back and walked over to her with a domineering demeanor. "You will never understand it until it is *time* for it to be revealed. *I* wouldn't question the Powers That Be as to why they chose Cassi. Perhaps *you* would like to ask them yourself."

"What?"

"Come."

Rick took her arm harshly, turned to James, and gave him a look of pure delight. Dominique's eyes widened as a bolt of electricity surged through her body. It started at her feet and worked its way up, until her eyes went piercingly white. She was falling, but could still feel Rick's hand coolly on her arm. The feeling ended in an abrupt snap of unnerving power.

When she regained her ability to see, Dominique found herself standing alone in a small room. The walls were like translucent glass, the universe seeming only inches past the walls. When she touched the glass, it sang out in a beautiful symphony of sound. Light darted from her fingertips as she lightly brushed the cool surface, causing immaculate tones to form from its towering walls.

"What do you want, mortal?" a voice boomed over the music.

Dominique jumped, her hand falling from the glass, ending the run of its tone in what could be considered an ending to a masterpiece. When Dominique looked around her, no one was with her in the cramped room.

"Answer me."

Dominique looked puzzled, peering through the walls to find the voice before she answered, "Where am I?"

"In a room that the entire universe was created in, a blank starting point for the gods to create nothing and everything."

"Are you the Powers That Be?"

"Perhaps."

"Well, if you are, then I guess I'm supposed to ask you why you picked Cassi to be the chosen one," Dominique replied.

"For the same reason we chose you."

Dominique was more confused. "Huh?" she asked.

There was a sigh. "You mortals who think you understand the world always need to have every detail explained. You are a slayer, chosen to represent the world of good on the planet to which you are born. So why were you chosen to be a slayer, this representation, when obviously you are not the best choice for the challenge?"

Dominique wasn't sure how to take that comment. "I don't know. That's why I asked you."

"Fate has a way with things. We decide fate. That question is one that will be revealed to you in a time that has been already set in stone, a time that not even I can change."

"If you decide fate, then who influences your decisions?"

"You."

"*I* influence *you*? That doesn't seem likely."

"Each person influences his or her own life. It is only when their choices remove the power of another that the balance is affected, and then we must step in."

"And vampires take the choice away from other

people, so that is why I have been born," Dominique said, beginning to understand.

"That is why slayers are born, but why you were born is a totally different matter, or perhaps is the same matter altogether. That portion of your life will not be determined until a time in the near future."

"I'm sorry, what?"

"You will understand shortly. That is the point, the point of your questions, the point of the Protector sending you to me, the point of your life, and the point of your dreams. This reminds me, I believe there is someone who would like to speak with you."

"You're worse than Horus. Now I know where he gets it. Who wants to speak with me now?"

"Well, that is the interesting part. In a way, she is you. I believe she is the person you play in your dreams: Isis."

"Who is Isis?" Dominique asked.

The being sighed again. "So poorly informed. She is the mother of this world. Married to the god Osiris, and in symbol, she is your sister..." the voice silenced.

The glass around Dominique became exceedingly bright as a pillar descended around her. There was no place for her to escape the light. All she could do was peer into the glass. Amidst the light, she began to make out the faint figure of someone in a white robe. The figure's eyes slowly became visible. They were blue, very pale, but powerful. Her white skin was more like ivory. The robe she wore cradled her. She was full of light, even more so than Horus.

"Turn around and meet me," the figure stated at the

moment when Dominique realized she was peering at a reflection in the glass.

When Dominique turned around, this woman was standing in the room with her. "Who are you?" Dominique asked, with a slight bow, not able to think of anything else to do or say.

"I am Isis, your mother, your sister, and your friend. Hear me. I am to answer the question that has been puzzling your mind. It is time. Ask. I cannot answer if you do not ask."

"You have been in my dreams. I am… I am you in these dreams?"

"That is correct."

"Why?"

"Now that is quite a story. Come, and I will show you," Isis stated, and then putting her arm gently around Dominique, she began chanting. "Oh my sister, gather around me that I may tell the tale of the Before-Time, of the Golden Age when the gods walked upon the earth with men. Know then, that in those ancient days, long before even the grandfather of our Pharaoh's grandfather was born, Osiris, the great-grandson of Ra, sat upon the throne of the gods, ruling over the living world as Ra did over the gods. He was the first Pharaoh, and I was the first queen. We ruled for many ages together, for the world was still young and Grandmother Death was not as harsh as she is now.

"His ways were just and upright; he made sure that Maat remained in balance, that the law was kept. And so Maat smiled upon the world. All people praised Osiris, and peace reigned over all, for this was the Golden Age.

"Yet there was trouble. Proud Set, noble Set, the brother of Osiris, he who defended the Sun Boat from Apep the Destroyer, was unsettled in his heart. He coveted the throne of Osiris. He coveted me. He coveted the power over the living world, and he desired to take it from his brother. In his dark mind he conceived of a plot to kill Osiris and take all from him. He built a box and inscribed it with wicked magic that would chain anyone who entered it from escaping.

"Set took the box to the great feast of the gods. He waited until Osiris had made himself drunk on much ale, and then challenged Osiris to a contest of strength. Each one in turn would enter the box and attempt, through sheer strength, to break it open. Osiris, sure in his power, yet feeble in mind because of his drink, entered the box. Set quickly poured molten lead into the box. Osiris tried to escape, but the wicked magic held him bound and he died. Set then picked up the box and hurled it into the Nile where it floated away.

"Set claimed the throne of Osiris for himself and demanded that I be his queen. None of the other gods dared to stand against him, for he had killed Osiris and could easily do the same to them. Great Ra turned his head aside and mourned, but he did not stand against Set.

"This was the dark time. Set was everything his brother was not. He was cruel and unkind, caring not for the balance of Maat, or for me, or for you. War divided Egypt, and all was lawless while Set ruled. In vain our people cried to Ra, but his heart was hardened by grief, and he would not listen.

"Only I remembered the children of the world. Only I was unafraid of Set. I searched all of the Nile for the box containing my beloved husband. Finally I found it, lodged in a tamarisk bush that had turned into a mighty tree, for the power of Osiris was still in him, though he lay dead. I tore open the box and wept over the lifeless body of Osiris. I carried the box back to Egypt and placed it in the house of the gods. I changed myself into a bird and flew about his body, singing a song of mourning. Then I perched upon him and cast a spell. The spirit of dead Osiris entered me, and I conceived and bore a son whose destiny it would be to avenge his father. I called the child Horus and hid him on an island far away from the gaze of his uncle Set.

"I then went to Thoth, wise Thoth who knows all secrets, and implored his help. I asked him for magic that could bring Osiris back to life. Thoth, lord of knowledge, who brought himself into being by speaking his name, searched through his magic. He knew that Osiris's spirit had departed his body and was lost. To restore Osiris, Thoth had to remake him so that his spirit would recognize him and rejoin his body. Thoth and I together created the Ritual of Life, that which allows us to live forever when we die. But before Thoth could work the magic, cruel Set discovered us. He stole the body of Osiris and tore it into pieces, scattering them throughout Egypt. He was sure that Osiris would never be reborn.

"Yet I would not despair. I implored the help of my sister Nephthys, kind Nephthys, to guide me and help me find the pieces of Osiris. Long did we search, bringing each piece to Thoth that he might work magic upon it. When all the pieces were together, Thoth went to Anubis, lord of the dead. Anubis sewed the pieces back together, washed the entrails of Osiris, embalmed him, wrapped him in linen, and cast the Ritual of Life. When Osiris's mouth was opened, his spirit reentered him and he lived again.

"Yet nothing that has died, not even a god, may dwell fully in the land of the living. Osiris went to Duat, the abode of the dead. Anubis yielded the throne to him, and he became the lord of the dead. There he stands in judgment over the souls of the dead. He commends the just to the Blessed Land, but the wicked he condemns to be devoured by Ammit.

"When Set heard that Osiris lived again he was wroth, but his anger waned, for he knew that Osiris could never return to the land of the living. Without Osiris, Set believed he would sit on the throne of the gods for all time. Yet on his island, Horus, who you know as Rick, the son of Osiris and I, grew to manhood and strength. Set sent many serpents and demons to kill Horus, but he defeated them all. When he was ready, I gave him great power to use against Set, and Thoth gave him a magic knife.

"Horus sought out Set and challenged him for the throne. Set and Horus fought for many days, but in the end Horus defeated Set and castrated him. But Horus, merciful Horus, would not kill Set, for to spill the blood of his uncle would make him no better than he. Set maintained his claim to the throne, and Horus lay claim himself as the son of Osiris. The gods began to fight amongst one another, those who supported Horus and those who supported Set. Banebdjetet leaped into the middle and demanded that the gods end this struggle peacefully or Maat would become further imbalanced. He told the gods to seek the council of Neith. Neith, warlike though wise in council, told them that Horus was the rightful heir to the throne. Horus cast Set into the darkness where he lives to this day.

"And so it is that Horus watches over us while we live and gives guidance to the Pharaoh while he lives, and his father Osiris watches over us in the next life. So it is that the gods are at peace. So it is that Set, wicked Set, eternally strives for revenge, battling Horus at every turn. When Horus wins, Maat is upheld and the world is at peace. When Set wins, the world is in turmoil. But we know that dark times do not last forever, and the bright rays of Horus will shine over us again.*

"It is in attempt to win his battle with Horus that Set sought out Judas, he who became the first vampire. Do you know that story?"

Dominique answered, "I don't know any story that has Judas and a vampire in it. I have heard stories of the first vampire, but please, tell me?"

This made Isis smile, and as she did, if it were possible, the room became even brighter. "I will describe that Judas Iscariot, he who betrayed Jesus the Christ, became the first and head of the vampires. I will do this with some help from a book of scripture. Have you ever read the Bible?"

Dominique rolled her eyes. "I'm sorry, not really."

Isis's face remained emotionless. "The Bible, in a

seemingly contradictory manner, discusses the death of Judas the apostle in two accounts. The first account says, 'And he cast down the pieces of silver in the temple, and departed, and went and hanged himself,' while another reads, '…and falling headlong, he burst asunder in the midst, and all his bowels gushed out.' The great secret is that both are correct. According to the first scripture, found in Matthew 27:1, a conversation pursued between Judas and those to whom he sold the Lamb of God. He later, according to Acts, purchased a plot of land with the silver coins, which were his price for Christ. Because of his guilt, at sunset, he hung himself on a tree. The hanging, however, did not cause instant death, and Judas was still alive as the sun set. As the last ray of light danced on the horizon, the rope that suspended Judas mysteriously broke, causing him to fall and his bowels to gush out. He was dead, because his soul went to what you might call Purgatory. He was not dead, because his life force combined with the spirit summoned to him by his act of betraying Christ, was still found in his body. Because of this, a term was coined, one by which vampires are often referred: they are *undead*.

"And so it is, that wooden stakes can harm vampires, in symbol of the tree that suspended the living Judas. As though the tree couldn't finish its job in the time past, it comes with more force in the hand of the slayer in the form of a stake. Vampires can also be defeated by beheading, finishing the job of the noose. A silver cross is a reminder of the silver that betrayed the Christ and the cross on which he suffered for the pains of the world, including those of Judas. Again, it also helps us to understand why a young vampire cannot walk in the light of day, unless Maat becomes unbalanced in favor of wickedness, because it was only after the last ray of day that Satan was able to exercise his power in the supernatural breaking of the suspending rope. Sun charges life and brings about the needs of the world. Vampires are not alive, and in the light, the sun burns their dead flesh. Experience, however, can overrule this great desire of life. Older vampires find it possible to walk in the light of day, but it is uncomfortable and challenging. Most see no reason to abandon their shadows to the light. Set has never seen the day since he was changed, and he prefers it that way.

"The good forces of the world, in order to counter evil's attacks, called the first slayer. This is a role that I took upon myself. You see, we are sisters. We are both slayers. It was my calling to succeed in the killing of the mortal body of Judas Iscariot, which sealed his spirit in Purgatory, where Osiris condemned him to Ammit. Of course that didn't happen until he had already changed that wicked Set into one like him.

"It was the thirst for power that caused Set to seek out Judas. Horus had trapped him in the darkness, but Set didn't care; he wanted nothing but power. The change of this god caused quite a shift in the underworld. Osiris never saw the soul of Set; yet he was dead. Set could now walk the earth, defying all powers of the gods, for the dead are not supposed to be allowed to walk the earth. It is this power, the power to defy the gods, which Set sought. He now fights Horus from his darkness and has the ability to call upon others, turn them into one like himself, and build an army.

"It is now your job to ensure Set is slain. It is per prophecy that he is to perish during your reign as slayer. But, and you'll have to forgive me for interfering, fate is attempting to resolve this war. As Isis, the mother of this world, and mother of Horus, I have an ending of my own in mind. I cannot change fate any more than Horus can, but I believe I have information that will change the outcome of this battle. That is what I am attempting to tell you with these stories. I will go to Set. What you do is up to you. Remember that he is to be slain during your lifetime. Do your job, nothing more. Now you know. Use this knowledge well."

The light became dark, and the glass around Dominique turned opaque. "Wait!" she said, but the ground waved like water, and Dominique was plunged into it. The tunnel she was falling down was dark, and she saw stars burning past her as time began to slow down. No, it wasn't slowing down, time was normal now. Then a bright light approached quickly, expanding and growing brighter. When she entered the light she immediately jolted back into life. Suddenly, she was back in Cynthia's house, on Cynthia's couch.

She groaned and put her hand on her aching head. She rolled over, catching Cynthia's eyes. "How long have I been out?"

"Three days," Cynthia answered.

"Geez, it felt like I was only gone for fifteen minutes!"

Cynthia yawned. "You up for a little slaying? I've been bored waiting for you to wake up."

Dominique sat up, peering at her. "I actually feel quite rested; why are you so eager to go out?"

"I found a vamp nest."

"Where?"

"A small church just south of here."

"Let's go."

CHAPTER THIRTEEN

The sun fell gently behind the mountains to the west. Cynthia and Dominique already stood waiting outside the chapel door. Cynthia could feel the anticipation rise in her stomach, a feeling that often accompanied her when she was going on a major slay. She knew that with Dominique, she could easily take the number of vampires that were waiting beyond the chapel door. The air grew cold as the horizon darkened. Dusk had come, inviting the evil that contained itself within the church to come forth.

Dominique looked at Cynthia, her lips curling mischievously. With quiet prowess, she carefully pulled open the door, exposing the interior to the small amount of sunlight that still stained the sky. There was a roar, and an object just inside the doorway burst into flames.

"You would think the young ones would learn not to sleep next to the door," Dominique whispered.

Cynthia laughed.

"That sounded like nervous laughter," Dominique stated, pushing the door closed again. "You okay?"

Cynthia shrugged. "I'll be fine. I always get a little nervous during a slay this big. We don't even know how many vamps are in there."

"We can take them. We'll watch each others' backs."

The disturbance of light was contained in the vestibule, the major cathedral still one door away. The vampire's body finished fueling the flames, and a pile of dust remained where the previously sleeping vampire had met his fate. Dominique stomped disrespectfully on the pile, sending the dust high into the air and scattering its remains throughout the room. "Go toward the light…" she said ghoulishly.

The last beam of light flashed, fighting to last forever before it was consumed in the darkness of night. Dominique and Cynthia had now been waiting, not daring to wake the vampires, wanting them to be rested enough to put up a good fight. After all, the fight was half the fun.

Finally, the slayers heard the gentle sound of stirring. Their eyes widened as they realized that there had to be at least twenty vampires in the small chapel. The two girls looked at one another, nodded, and with a curdling scream, pulled open the double doors to expose the unsuspecting vampires.

The faces of the undead twisted as they realized that someone had discovered their nest.

"You know that a church is a sacred place," Cynthia announced. "You should be careful sleeping here; holy water does funny things to beings like you."

The numerous vampires sneered, exposing their pointed teeth. Dominique's adrenaline was pumping as she slapped holy water from a font into the crowd. It caught two of the vampires, causing them to burst into flames as though they had been staked through their hearts.

The others charged, immediately overtaking the two slayers. The slayers enjoyed the quick-paced battle, as with every thrust of their stakes, a vampire dissolved into dust at their feet. The heat of the battle was intense. Cynthia kept her back pressed firmly to Dominique's as she fought, trusting her friend to ensure that there would be no surprises. The only surprise came when the attack suddenly ended. Two vampires headed for the corner, while the others beat their way past the slayers and into the open night.

"There are only two in here; you take them," Dominique commanded. "I'll follow the ones outside."

Cynthia obeyed, walking deeper into the chapel. She saw the two vampires taking refuge behind a larger-than-life-sized statue of Mother Mary. Cynthia could hear them breathing in small growls, inviting her toward them. She smiled to herself, feeling she was going to enjoy this. She stepped forward, listening to her own feet hit the cold floor. Mother Mary now loomed above her, her eyes dark, protective, as if this symbol of good was repenting for serving as a shelter for such pure evil. Cynthia hated it, the feeling that good supported evil, and she knew that it was just the evil attempting to overpower the good. Evil would fail.

The doors behind Cynthia slammed shut so thunderously that Cynthia shuddered. She spun around, expecting the wind to be the assailant, but she could feel another presence in the room—a presence of absolute hatred. At first she thought she saw only a shadow, but she quickly realized it was a force, a man, a beast. Its head was covered in a black veil, hiding the creature's face in shadows that jumped off the walls to greet it. The being exposed his hand, and the candles in the room burst into flame. Cynthia watched, mesmerized and confused. The beast pulled the cloak from his body slowly, finally exposing his face.

"Perhaps you have heard of me," he spoke. "I am the father of darkness, the heir to the throne of evil."

"Lucas," Cynthia stated coolly, though her head was whirling.

Lucas bowed gracefully.

"Where is Cassi?"

"She is safe."

"Liar."

He tilted his head. "I don't lie."

"You are the father of lies."

His face twisted. "Actually, that would be the one my father serves. It seems you misunderstand the hierarchy."

Cynthia struggled under his glare. He approached her slowly until she could feel his hot breath bearing down on her. She saw her moment and raised her stake.

He reacted quickly, blocking her blow and hitting her with a quick backhand. He laughed. The vampires that had hidden behind the saintly statue now exposed themselves, rushing to aid their master.

"Go help your brothers with the other slayer," Lucas commanded. "This is my fight."

They obeyed, scrambling into the night through the nearest exit.

He then turned to Cynthia, "You're going to have to be much faster with that stake. I believe in fairness. I will let you go now, if you choose. Run, slayer! Run into the night. Grant me the pleasure of knowing that I scare you."

"And if I stay?" Cynthia questioned.

Lucas paused, gave a half smirk that exposed one of his sharp fangs. "Then I *will* scare you... to death."

Cynthia stood firm. The Protector had warned her about this particular evil, but she was unable to leave this battle; this conflict was her destiny. She smiled, laughed, and invited him closer to her. He took her offer and swung a quick right fist. Cynthia blocked, took hold of his strong arm, and flipped Lucas over her small shoulder, sending him crashing down on the wooden pews. He grunted in pain as wood splintered into his chest, barely missing his heart.

"For that you will pay with your life," he hissed.

"You can't do much to me while lying there," Cynthia replied, not ready to finish this fight by killing him.

"Is your goal to try to kill me?" Lucas asked.

"I don't need to try."

He jumped quickly, balancing all four limbs before he sprang to his full height. He was now directly square with Cynthia. His huge shoulders towered above the small slayer.

Cynthia laughed as she swung her left fist. The vampire blocked, so she immediately followed with her right, satisfied as it connected with his cheekbone. He returned the blow with a quick slap, his razor-sharp fingernails slashing her cheek, causing a steady stream of blood to drip from the wound.

Cynthia jumped back, avoiding another blow, kicking her right foot. Lucas caught it, and Cynthia jumped, kicking at his gripping hands with her left. She connected, causing him to lose his grip and balance. Both the slayer and the vampire fell to the ground. They looked at each other for a moment before they moved, each pair of eyes filled with hate and fear.

They recovered quickly, each using their natural gifts to try and regain equilibrium before the other did. Lucas succeeded in finding his balance first. He shoved Cynthia with great force, causing her to return to the ground, sprawling as she slid into a wall.

"Ouch," she cried out as her back buckled against the wooden trim that decorated the wall.

Lucas picked up a pew from the rows that filled the chapel and thrust it at her. Cynthia rolled as the pew shattered a stained glass window, causing fragments of broken glass to fall in shards around her.

Cynthia stood, brushing the dirt from her pants. "You got my capris dirty. That one is going to cost you."

She pulled a wooden stake from her belt and watched as Lucas's eyes followed the pointed edge. She thrust it with amazing speed and accuracy. Lucas caught the stake an instant before it would have penetrated his heart.

"This is Father's cloak that you just punctured a hole in, my dear. I'm done playing; your end has come."

"Bring it on."

Lucas lunged forward and pulled Cynthia down by her fine black hair. She cried out as chunks of scalp ripped from her skull. Cynthia found her revenge in a quick back kick, sending Lucas to the ground. As he stood, Cynthia lunged, a stake in hand. But she was too late; he had already regained his balance. Lucas caught Cynthia midair, spinning her around, pinning her against his own body. She struggled, but his massive arms held her. He carried her to the statue whose eyes helplessly witnessed the horror that was taking place. Mary's arms were outstretched, reaching toward Cynthia, perhaps attempting to free her, perhaps wanting to restrain her, perhaps trying to warn her.

Lucas set Cynthia's feet on the ground, but still held her against her will. She felt his nose brush her neck, his breath burn her skin. She cried out as she felt his chiseled teeth softly press into her skin.

"No!" she cried. "If tonight is to be my night, please not like this."

Lucas removed his fangs, and Cynthia thought for a moment that perhaps he was going to release her. Then suddenly his grip tightened, the full weight of his body pushing the air out of Cynthia's lungs. As she struggled for breath she saw his eyes out of the corner of her own. They were looking at her, calm, collected, cool, and heartless.

His view then shifted as his eyes came to rest on the statue of Mary. The lighted candles around the saint made her face glow with a brilliant luminescence. Her rosy cheeks shone serenely on a forgiving face. Her head was tilted, and the garments she wore undulated upon her like deep water, their blue hue reflected in Cynthia's frightened eyes.

Lucas studied the face, the clothing, the statue with its arms outstretched toward him—his saving grace. He then looked at Cynthia again, a quick glance back to the statue, then to Cynthia, and finally, his gaze fell on Mary's eyes.

"Forgive me, Father, for I have sinned," he whispered with an odd sound of sincerity.

His hands then enveloped Cynthia's head, and after a quick twist, a lethal snap echoed through the chapel. Cynthia uttered a slight groan before the chapel went silent, and the mortally wounded slayer collapsed.

Lucas placed Cynthia's body into the open arms of Mary and carefully adjusted the slayer so she appeared to be resting comfortably in the loving protection of God. Finally, he turned to leave, wearing an expression of strangely mixed sadness and gratification.

CHAPTER FOURTEEN

Dominique's teeth clenched. If she weren't using the self-control her slayer instincts gave her, she would undoubtedly be sobbing. Her eyes brimmed with tears despite her efforts, causing black streaks of mascara to trail unwillingly down her cheeks. Music rang from the organ, its sweet, soft tones forbidding Dominique to escape from her emotions, not even for a moment. Light fell lazily through the overhead windows, casting unnerving shadows across the chapel floor. This was not the church he had murdered Cynthia in; instead, it was a quaint Latter-day Saint building, quiet and humble. James and the other pallbearers lifted the dark oak casket and carried it to the awaiting hearse.

There were no dry eyes in this room filled with drooping flowers. Dominique knew that Cynthia was liked. The small sanctuary was filled to capacity, but the room still felt empty. Dominique and Cynthia had shared something special, something that no one here could understand.

Cynthia's parents huddled together in a corner. A mass of friends and family surrounded and consoled them in their grief. Dominique, however, had no one. She couldn't bear to be here any longer, so she burst through the chapel doors and into the fading sunlight. She gave her friend's casket one last glance as the pallbearers lifted it into the hearse, and said a whispered goodbye.

The walk home was well over ten miles, but Dominique had company. James walked silently behind her. Cars sped by them on the road, the drivers never asking or caring to give them a ride. Dominique felt more than ever like a nobody, cared for by no one and with no one to care for.

The sun fell, slipping to the other side of the world with another beautifully colored show, but Dominique didn't care. She ignored the sunset as she always did, never taking time to appreciate what she had until it was gone.

James caught up with her, touched her arm lightly, and pulled it over his own. She caught his eyes for an instant whenever the passing headlights hit them, and she could see that he, too, was struggling to hold in his emotions. James understood Dominique's loss more than most, but would never fully understand what the friendship of another slayer had meant to Dominique.

The air grew cold as the city lights reached toward the walking friends. Hours had passed before they entered Cynthia's home. Even though Dominique was uncomfortable here, always expecting Cynthia to come bounding through the door, she remained. Cynthia's parents were staying with relatives, giving the group of grieving friends a few more nights alone in the house that held so many memories for them. Dominique decided that the fun that she had had before this tragedy occurred was now a part of the past; vengeance was now not only desirable, but a requirement. She caught her own reflection in a hallway mirror. Her face was still streaked in black, but she had matured in the days since Cynthia's murder. Now the fire in her eyes burned with renewed intensity. Her face grew hot, and she realized for the first time in several days that she was famished. Her hunger consumed her like the darkness that was consuming the world. Yet, this was not a hunger for food, but for revenge. The thought crossed her mind that in her quest to avenge Cynthia, innocent people could get hurt, but she blocked her compassion and replaced it with indifference for anyone or anything that stood in the way of revenge.

The large, front room window revealed a sky full of burning stars. They seemed to reproach Dominique, reprimanding her, betraying her. In the heavens, a bright light flashed as though a new star had just burst into existence. Dominique saw it from the window and said nothing, thought nothing, and made no movement. Another light burst closer to the house, enveloped it, and blinded those contained therein. When Dominique's eyes adjusted, Rick stood before them, dressed in radiant gold. He looked at her without a smile. He paced to his favorite chair, looked at it, then paced back to the center of the room only to return again. Finally he sat.

Dominique was furious. "You let her die," she said, the first words escaping from her mouth in over three hours.

"No, I let *you* live. Fate has decreed what fate—"

"Don't give me fate! My best friend died."

"So that you could live."

"What?"

"Are you aware, Dominique, that there is only one slayer in the world? One. Single. Alone. Never have there been two, and the slayer is only called where she is needed most."

"So let me guess; fate just balanced itself. Is that it? Is that supposed to make me feel better?"

"You are sorely incorrect. I called two slayers. I interfered with fate. Now that two slayers have lived on the same planet, that choice cannot be undone. With Cynthia's death, another slayer will be called. There will be two slayers on this planet forevermore. However, just like the case of you and Cynthia, one will be the primary, the first-called, while the other will simply be... less."

Dominique paused, her mind twisting between anger and hate. Then through clenched teeth she asked, "Who was the first slayer called?"

The Protector looked up and smiled for the first time that evening. "The one who survived, of course."

"Wait. I thought you called me here, and that is where our problems with fate started in the first place. Cynthia was already here, and had been her entire life."

"Cynthia was called from birth by me as were you. I knew this battle could not be won alone, so shortly after your birth I found another girl with potential. This has taken a long time to prepare. You were asked to come from the place you were most needed, to the place where I most needed you."

Everything was clouded in Dominique's mind, but she didn't care. "I wasn't supposed to be moved from Seattle? Cynthia shouldn't have been a slayer at all? I have you all figured out," she said.

"Really?" he asked.

Dominique's anger grew. It was his fault that Cynthia was killed, so that she, Dominique, could live. He called Cynthia to be a slayer. He knew this battle couldn't be won with just one slayer, so he called another, knowing all along that this other slayer would die! The *other* slayer would die, instead of the *only* slayer dying. Cynthia was his *sacrifice!* Dominique felt sick. She pointed accusingly at Rick and shook her head in disbelief. "I'm going to kill her. I'm going to make Lucas watch as I push a wooden stake through his bride's heart. Then I will make him suffer, ending it all by mixing his blood with hers. Let them spend an eternity in hell together if they wish…"

"You will be stopped."

"Oh, yes. Your little prophesies. You are supposed to save the world from its 'black roots,' but you can no longer interfere with fate. You can't stop me!" Dominique said, turning toward the door.

"It is not your fate to end their lives. Do you remember your first day here? You asked me a question about free will and why bad things happen to good people. I could not interfere."

"Well I can."

"Fate will stop you, too."

"Don't lie to me. I spoke with The Powers That Be, remember? Hmm? You sent me there. Your mother told me I will choose my path, and that my fate will be written accordingly. Now, I choose a life without you."

"You misinterpreted."

Dominique stared at him coldly. Fire flew from her eyes in a look that made Rick uncomfortable. Her biceps knotted into large balls the size of her clenched fists. For a moment she looked like she was going to strike him. Restraining herself, she turned and headed for the door.

"I cannot let you leave," Rick said, and the door locks clicked shut.

Dominique turned to him, smiled wryly, grasped the handle, and with the strength she knew she had, pulled the door completely off its hinges, leaving a broken doorframe and an opening to the shadowy world in its place. Her shoes clicked like sharp stilettos as she strolled calmly down the walkway.

"One more task completed," Rick said to a bewildered James, who had come racing down the stairs when he heard the screaming. Upon seeing the heated exchange, he had hidden himself around a corner, within earshot.

He looked confused as he stepped out of his hiding place, positioning himself on the couch. "You *meant* to make her angry at you?"

"I'm tired of waiting. Dominique's anger will lead her to the final battle more quickly, and will also give her the extra strength she needs to defeat evil."

"So, did you lie to her?" James asked.

The Protector shook his head. "I told the truth on every account."

"Then you did mean for Cynthia to die?"

Rick sighed. "I didn't want her to fall. As time progressed, I did know that her end was coming. I didn't know when or how, but because of the call I issued, I knew her end would come sooner than was fair. She knew it too. I believe she had it revealed to her some time ago. She knew it long before I did. She couldn't win against Lucas, and she knew that."

"So then it is Dominique's fate to destroy Cassi and Lucas?"

"I believe it is going to be slightly more complex than that. I see glimpses of what is to come, and it is not Dominique we need to be concerned with."

"Yet she left our circle," James stated. "How can we defend the world without a slayer?"

"We haven't lost our slayer. She just thinks we have."

A pale light began to emerge, bringing brightness to the skies. James breathed heavily as it glowed over the mountains. Suddenly he sat straight up. He stood and ran down the hallway, paying careful attention to the windows in the house. When he returned, he carried a compass in his hands. He looked at it, then outside, then at the compass again. He shifted his gaze to Rick, who was sitting calmly, watching the sunrise. "Am I crazy?" James said. "Am I seeing things?"

"No," Rick responded.

"Why is the sun rising in the west?"

Rick shifted his focus from the window to James. "Once per millennia, the powers of good are thwarted; the balance is overthrown, and the world is turned upside down. This physical event is a sign. The balance of Maat is overthrown. Evil is winning."

James gawked.

"How good do you think you would be at slaying vampires?" Rick asked.

"It isn't our job to slay the vampires."

Rick just looked at him blankly.

"Depends on how well I warm up my powers," James responded.

"I suggest you start. The balance of Maat has been affected. With the world tipped, the sun is unable to aid in the growth of life. The vampires will be out today, and although it is Dominique's job to slay them, she will need our help."

***

The day moved frantically for everyone, including Rick and James. They had their hands full jumping from place to place, destroying vampires who had come out to experience the strange new light. The evil of the world rejoiced, and even seemed eager when the Protector approached them. Their pale skin set them apart from the mere mortals—the alabaster skin that seemed to glow more eerily now than at night.

Rick disliked the way he was forced to slay. Often people watched as he and James destroyed a life, or what the mortals thought was a life. They often used their powers to help those who were being attacked, but had to be careful to keep them from witnessing their special powers, or "magic" as some would term it. Rick needed to be especially careful to hide his true identity, though he doubted that many of the Pleasant Grove citizens had studied Egyptian legend and knew anything about him anyway.

Police cars lined the streets, picking up vampires that were seen attacking mortals. Often these well-meaning law enforcement men and women became victims themselves, as the small chains that made the handcuffs were no match for the vampires' strength, and guns no match for their agility. Mortal weapons were of no use at all, in fact, except for the wooden stake, which not many seemed to have handy.

Therefore, the world on this day was in chaos. James knew that Dominique had to be out there somewhere. Just because she and Rick had an argument didn't mean that she would shirk her responsibilities, or so James believed. His thoughts wandered from time to time, only to be pulled back into the present by Rick and the task at hand. Even Rick looked haggard, and James was beginning to feel the pressure himself. He was finding it difficult to focus his powers. Rick had warned him that practicing crafts would be tiring, but James had never imagined the depth of the fatigue he was now feeling.

It was noon when a familiar face approached them

on the street. She walked with a gun in hand, cocked and ready to fire. She then crouched, watching them from a strip of bushes that lined the outer boundary of a popular park. Rick noticed her prying eyes immediately, and even knew her intentions, but he was purposely more focused on the tasks that needed to be completed. He held a vampire while James thrust a stake into its heart.

The park was almost deserted now; the people had fled, and many vampires had been slain. James and Rick set off toward the outer park boundary, pushing the remaining vampires back toward their secret cavern, to their leader and Cassi. They passed the familiar figure still crouched in the bushes. Rick gave her a quick glance as they passed. He noticed that her eyes were bewildered and angry. No doubt she had no explanation for what was occurring. James noticed nothing. His eyes were closed as he walked down the straight path, attempting to get some type of rest from his weariness.

They turned a corner and paused, hearing footsteps behind them. The steps halted, and when James turned, an unsettling silence fell around him. Rick stared forward, not acknowledging their existence. Rick and James continued their slow walk toward a group of people in the distance. Their pace increased as the sound of the footsteps behind them returned. Rick knew who was following them; James was confused by the look on Rick's face.

Then, just off the sidewalk, hidden behind a row of trees, James heard a high-pitched cry and a low growl. He knew immediately that an attack had occurred just six feet from their position. James turned to step off the sidewalk into the trees, but Rick pulled him back.

"Don't."

"We've gotta go help," James whispered, looking deeply into Rick's frozen eyes. Rick nodded reluctantly and stepped into the brush with James.

They found a young girl, no more than ten years of age, lying in a small, grassy patch hidden by surrounding trees. Her neck had been pierced; two small wounds now bled slowly. Her eyes were white and glossy, her skull crushed with what James knew was the rock that lay next to the small girl's side. Rick bent over the body and brushed the girl's cheek.

"You will be rewarded in heaven for your choice young one," he whispered. "That was a brave thing you did."

James was silent. "If you weren't so reluctant, we could have saved her. Why did you hesitate? Why did you stop me?"

Rick pointed back toward the way they had come. James, angered, turned back to the trees.

"Freeze!" a booming voice commanded. James heard multiple guns click, loading empty chambers with deadly bullets. Rick looked up defiantly at the leader of the group of police officers. Officer Kendra Allred glared back at him, a deep hatred sparking in her eye. She had a slight smirk on her face, as though she had caught them in some indecent act that would ensure her a promotion. "You are under arrest," she continued, slapping handcuffs on Rick while another officer put handcuffs on James. "You have the right to remain silent; anything you say or do may be used against you in a court of law."

"You are making a mistake," Rick said.

"Tell it to that girl," Allred snapped, then to another officer, "This one is coming in my car."

"You've already got someone in your car," a gruff voice answered.

"A 'yes ma'am' would suffice," Allred barked, forcing Rick into the back of an already occupied car. Then instructing the current passenger she said, "You, get in the front."

The other person exited the car at Allred's request and was pushed roughly into the front seat despite Rick's angry glance. "Don't do this," Rick said softly as Allred slammed her door and started the car.

"Shut up! I'm sick of you people. I knew you were the one killing all those people around town. Finally we caught you in the act, in broad daylight!" She shifted into gear and floored the pedal.

The front seat passenger turned to Rick and smiled wryly.

"Watch yourself," Rick warned Allred as the passenger's face twisted. Allred pulled the car against the curb and turned to face Rick.

"Is that a threat?" she stated, in an explosion of anger.

"Yes," the passenger stated, ripping the seat belt off and lunging at the officer.

Allred screamed and pulled her gun from her strap as the large figure landed on top of her. She fired to no avail; the figure continued his attack.

The cuffs on Rick's hands flashed yellow as they melted away from his wrists. His hands freed, he turned to the grate that separated the front and back seats. With one blow it trembled and flew against the vampire's body, flinging him into the windshield. Another flash of light pierced his heart, and Allred was instantly covered in dust.

It was too late. Rick saw Allred's hand reach for her neck, and as she pulled her hand away, she was shocked at the blood that gushed from the wound. She coughed, vomiting blood, staining the interior of her car.

Rick climbed over the seats.

"Coming to finish the job?" Allred choked out.

Rick pressed his hand against Allred's neck and closed his eyes. Allred felt weightless, her eyes saw only bright white. Then the universe was before her face; the stars and planets flew past her at amazing speeds. It looked to her as though she was following a bright green ball of electricity. Just as she was about to catch up with it, she began falling.

She plummeted, watching the ball rise higher and higher until it was so small she could no longer see it. When she came back to her senses, she was no longer herself.

Her light brown hair was now beautifully white and hung around her neck, trailing down her body in two thick braids. She wore a white cloak that covered her head, and she rode upon a thick, white stallion. Her thoughts were in a frenzy as the sound of the horse's hooves pounded in her head. She was chasing someone, but she couldn't see them. They were too far ahead of her, probably hours ahead of her, already in the little town that she was approaching. It was a quiet little town, snuggled up against a great mountain. Yet, in the dark, the town looked sinister.

She heard screaming as she approached. Finally she had found him, tracked him down. He now lurked inside, terrorizing the inhabitants. Scotland, she was in Scotland. She had to hurry. Dawn was approaching in just an hour—she could feel it. He would be looking for a place to escape the heat of the day.

Kendra reared her stallion and crashed through the city gates. "Where is he?" she cried to a small group of children huddled together in fear.

"Town square! Town square!" they screamed, pointing.

"Get inside! He can't come in unless he's invited. Get inside and don't answer the door!"

Kendra dug her heals deep into the horse's ribs, causing him to lurch forward in a full gallop. She rode him bareback, her arms tightly wrapped around the horse's powerful neck—she didn't know she knew how to ride bareback.

The horse seemed to know exactly where it was going, and strangely enough, Kendra did too. It was as if this was a memory. She rounded a corner and found herself in the middle of town. The square was full of people, all angry, all with some sort of weapon. A few men carried torches; others wielded pitchforks. The women mostly carried swords that looked too large for their petite frames.

"He has taken too many of us already! We must find

him!" they cried.

But she already knew where he was. She could feel him. A few of the townsfolk noticed her, poised majestically on her steed. A hush came over the crowd as all eyes eventually turned to her.

"I must ask you to return to your homes," she stated calmly. "You must secure your doors and comfort your children. He cannot enter your houses without an invitation. You cannot kill him; you have neither the knowledge nor ability to do so."

"*You* know nothing," one cried from the crowd. "My brother was taken from his room while he slept. The beast came into his bedroom and murdered him!"

"You lie, mortal," Kendra replied. "Your brother was a drunk, and you left him to wander the streets."

"Fiend! You are with him!" the peasant screamed, throwing a pitchfork at her.

Kendra chuckled, caught the pitchfork in midair, spun it over her head, and pointed it back at the peasant. "You will all return to your homes!" she commanded, spinning the fork again, this time slamming its end into the ground. As she did, a shower of sparks burst from its tips, illuminating the darkness.

The townspeople scattered, perhaps because of fear, perhaps because they saw her power, and respected her wish to return to their homes.

Kendra dismounted from her horse, turned to it, and patted its cheek. "Wait for me by the gate."

Surprisingly, the horse lowered its head and bent its knee in the form of a bow, turned, and galloped away.

The square had grown eerily quiet; a small bubbling

fountain was the only sound permeating the still night air. Kendra walked across the square, under a bridge, and turned to find herself in front of a large church, topped with a beautiful stained glass window, in front of which stood an intricately carved Celtic cross. Even without seeing him, she knew he was watching her, probably from the eyes of Saint Peter, staring at her from the window. Vampires love churches. Churches are the only place they are always welcome, the only place that doesn't require an invitation to enter. All are welcome there.

Kendra climbed the winding stairs; she was calm, resolute. She had chased him now for months, and she knew that this night was the night that fate had decreed his death. She knew, because she had spoken to Them about it.

It was before her now—a solid, heavy wooden door. She could feel the evil that contained itself therein. The air around her was cold, the darkness heavy enough to be felt.

She pushed the door open.

"Isis," the darkness hissed. She now stood in the doorway, the weight of the blackness bearing down on her.

"Face me, Iscariot."

And Kendra watched as a battle ensued. It was not a physical battle, but more like a summer storm. Clouds of darkness were shattered by bursts of light, warm air colliding with the cold. The screams and groans echoed in her head like thunder while sweat dampened the floor like rain.

It happened just as she knew it would; the sun began to peak over the village, its trail of light beginning to pierce through the windows they fought beside, causing streams of color to fill the room. The light stung Judas, reaching for him, wanting to finish the job it wasn't able to do the night he betrayed the Christ. Judas pushed past Isis and bolted for the door, seeking refuge from the light in the inward darkness of this desecrated building.

But Isis did not falter. With a mighty tug she tore her braids from her scalp and let out a blood-curdling scream that made Judas hesitate for just long enough. Using her powers, her hair came alive, whipping around Judas's neck. With all her strength Isis pulled, pulled Judas around in front of the window. She charged, and pushed. The glass was broken, but she forgot about the cross. As she tumbled over Judas, she tripped over it, and falling over the edge, saw the ground rush up to meet her. The fall was far, but she didn't care if she died. Kendra didn't care that she was falling; she needed only to see if she was successful.

So she turned, midair, to see Judas, suspended by her hair. One end held his neck while the other held the cross. She had won. He hung by her hair and burst into flames in the sunlight.

She didn't hit the ground, but instead a cushioned car seat. She sprawled over it, as she had been a moment before, and her vision cleared.

She gasped and sat up, spitting at the taste of rusted blood in her mouth. "Did I die?" The car had no sign of damage; the upholstery was clean, the window without a crack. She touched her neck, surprised that there wasn't even a scratch where there had been two gaping holes.

It was all a dream, she thought, her mind trying to settle upon the most reasonable explanation.

"No, it wasn't," Rick said calmly, reading her thoughts.

"Did she die? Did I... I mean... Isis. Did she die?"

Rick smiled, "Actually, Isis is my mother, and I couldn't just let her die. Can you imagine a fall from a church killing a goddess of Egypt? No, she didn't die; I caught her before she hit the ground."

"Your mother? Caught her? Who are you?"

"One who fights for good, much like you."

"You can't fight for good. I fight for good. You're too young to even know what good truly is."

Rick chuckled. "That didn't stop you from thinking I was a murderer."

"People often find out what bad is, before they know to choose good."

"I'm not as young or inexperienced as I may seem. Truly, I am centuries old. I chose to fight for good a long time ago; you could even say I was born for it really. We *are* in a war, Kendra, and we must all be careful, for time is running out. I saved you this time, but your carelessness may put you into danger again. You must be careful with your knowledge of the existence of these creatures, or they will find you."

He turned from her confused gaze, toward the door. The latch came open, the door swung ajar, and Rick stepped out. With a snap of his fingers, James was standing next to him, dazed.

Allred looked confused, bewildered, but most of all angry about losing her captive. In spite of that, she turned to her car, twisted the key that brought it to life, and pulled into the street, exhaust billowing out behind her.

CHAPTER FIFTEEN

The sun set quietly over the eastern mountains. Night came quickly, without the dull evening that forces uneasiness to fall upon the face of the world. Instead, the world fell from a bright morning into almost instant darkness. This darkness invited those vampires who had not wished to venture out during the day to join their friends and family in celebration of a joyous occasion: evil was winning.

Lucas peered at Cassi through the eerie light that penetrated the cavern. "Are we really going to sit here all night?"

"What do you have in mind?" Cassi replied, a faint smile on her face.

"Let's go for a walk, eat, anything but sit here and stare at each other," he suggested.

"Do you have a problem staring at me?"

Lucas chortled. "Of course not, I'm just hungry."

Cassi nodded her head slightly and stood, her long black dress flowing behind her, descending as an ebony cloud to the cavern floor.

"I love it when you do that."

"What?" she asked, turning to catch his eyes.

"Stand so... well... like that."

She kissed him quickly and took his hand, hers far warmer than his. She turned to walk, holding folds of black material in her hand, while dragging him after her with the other. She was surprised when he quit walking after just a few steps and hung his head.

"What?" she said. "It was your idea to go out, so let's go."

"Have you thought more about my request yet?" Lucas blurted out, embarrassed to ask.

"Which request?" Cassi asked, knowing perfectly well while attempting to avoid answering.

"Marriage."

Cassi looked warmly at his face. "I want to, more than anything in the world, but something deep within me is reluctant, like I am not meant to live this life with you forever."

Lucas smiled in spite of his frustration. "What kind of life would you live if you say no? The same one, I tell you, just alone. I am your destiny, your soul mate. Even my father thinks so, the witches, the community of vampires; there is even a prophecy about us. Don't you see? We are meant to be."

Cassi's eyes narrowed, puzzled. "What prophecy?"

Lucas, catching his mistake, took her other hand. "Just that there will be two vampires who fall madly in love, get married, and have a wonderful time ruling the dark world forever," he covered.

"I'd like to read this prophecy," Cassi said with a smile.

"Perhaps when we return from our walk," Lucas said, realizing that he would have to make this a long walk, so she would have time to forget. Reading the prophecy may make her doubt his sincerity or make her angry. They were too close to what they had been fighting for now. Too close to lose it over a slip of the tongue.

Cassi bit her bottom lip teasingly. "Let's go then."

They headed for the exit of the immaculate cavern, crossing dark passageways and even darker individuals. The three witches looked especially perturbed this evening. As she walked past them, Cassi noticed that they were boiling something foul smelling in a dark caldron. They smirked at her as she passed, each one moving in perfect stride with the others. That made Cassi uncomfortable; if there were anything that could make her uneasy in the dark, it would be being alone with those three. As she fell out of their view, she heard them whisper angrily, "We do so much, and he repays us none. He is the Darkness, dark power's number one. Perhaps we will have to teach him a lesson. Pay him a visit."

Their words made Cassi uneasy. Not knowing who they were talking about made it worse.

Finally they entered a large, circular room where water could be heard dripping softly into pools beyond unknown walls, the steady erosion eternally forming deeper caverns and darker hallways. Cassi paused momentarily, taking in the spectacle around her. She had seen this room before, of course, but its magic and mystery gave her a new feeling now... as though she were home. The stalagmites and stalactites reaching toward each other also reached for her. She could feel the walls of the cavern enfold and embrace her; their spirit filled the vacuum that was left behind by her own lost soul. Yes, she loved it here.

The entrance was now only a short climb away through rocks and boulders. Lucas had already gone ahead, and Cassi could see him climb effortlessly around a large rock and disappear, only to be seen again in the moonlight that marked a small crack, the entrance to their home. It was invisible to the rest of the world, so small that it couldn't be noticed from even a few feet away. Even if someone did see it they would surely never believe that the entrance led to an endless series of twisted passages and hundreds of large rooms.

Lucas turned and waited for Cassi to clamber over the trail until she took his awaiting hand in hers. They stepped into the starlight together, breathing deeply in the open air.

The night was cool; a slight, warm breeze enfolded the town in a sea of bliss. Cassi overlooked the field that stretched in front of them, the wind rippling the blades of grass and tossing pollen into the air. She smiled for no reason and realized that for the first time in eighteen years, she had just smiled because she was content.

Lucas dropped his hand from Cassi's and sprinted into the field, performing all sorts of childish jumps and turns, laughing in spite of himself. "The night is beautiful," he finally said, holding his hand out inviting her to join him.

Cassi did. As she ran to meet him her dress billowed behind her, making it appear as if she flew inches above the ground. Her glide ended with Lucas picking her up and dropping her affectionately on the grass. He fell on top of her, her hands above her head, him pinning her to the ground. "You're going to marry me, you know," he said, following with a deep, sacred kiss.

When the kiss was over, Cassi cried with a giggle, "Get off of me, you crazy freak!"

Lucas, with a smug look on his face, taunted her, "Make me."

Cassi's eyes squinted; she smiled and shoved, her vampire abilities giving her strength to send him sprawling on the grass ten feet from her. "Look, now I have grass stains on my dress and everything," she said, standing and dusting herself off. A disgruntled growl made her peer upwards.

"Run!" Lucas barked, only his hands visible in the tall grass. Cassi could see plainly why the mood had changed and why she was suddenly filled with fear. There, wrestling with Lucas, was a person Cassi now knew as the slayer—the one she had once only known as Dominique.

"Go!" Lucas shouted. Dominique's focus shifted to Cassi; her eyes glowed in the darkness with a strange animal-like fire. Cassi gasped, turned, and ran toward the cavern. She could hear soft footsteps pelting behind her, gaining quickly. Her dress caught on bushes, rocks, and grass, whatever it could to betray her.

I'm too slow, Cassi thought. Dominique would catch up to her in an instant.

She could hear Dominique's footsteps, and Dominique's hot breath pulsed down her neck. She ran with all her might, the safety of the cavern just seconds away. Suddenly she was falling, her fatigued legs unwilling to move any faster than her tense body. *I'm done for*, Cassi thought as she saw the ground approaching fast.

"Ouch!" she let out as she tumbled over herself, through the cavern entrance, and down the rocky path, plunging into darkness. Her body rolled and bounced off rocks of every size until finally she sprawled across the smooth floor of the open cavern below. Cassi forced herself to stand and continued to run deeper into the cavern, even though she no longer heard Dominique chasing her.

Finally, when Cassi reached the main cavern, she slumped against the mountainous wall, listening as she competed with the flames in the room for oxygen.

Dominique lost interest in Cassi as soon as she disappeared into the dark mountainside. Her slayer instinct told her to return her focus to Lucas, who must now be buried somewhere within the grass. Her feet had beaten the grass into a flat path as she chased Cassi, and she was able to follow this path carefully back to where Lucas's imprint was still fresh in the weeds. Dominique glanced around her, her hand resting on her head. There was too much grass for her to search alone, and Dominique doubted that Lucas was going to stick around for long, while his *love* was alone and shaken up inside their *castle*. Dominique, angry and unsatisfied, left the field and started the short walk back to town.

***

The air was stale. Dominique saw lightning in the distance from an incoming storm that moved slowly. No wind announced its arrival. She sat on a large rock on a grassy patch between two streets that marked the center of town. She drew up her legs and laid her cheek against her knees.

Her eyes rested momentarily, the only sound that of distant voices and her breath hot on her own flesh.

Suddenly her silence was interrupted with a loud bang that echoed through the sky. *Thunder,* she thought sleepily to herself. But a flash followed that in no way resembled lightning, almost forcing Dominique off her perch. Distant voices turned to screaming, and Dominique ran toward them. They echoed off the mountains, originating from the small stretch of nightclubs on the other side of town. When Dominique approached, she saw a wall of people with multiple piercings and spiked hair. They surrounded an innocent-looking female, who now lay cold on the cement.

Dominique pushed her way through the crowd; some people were frantic while others found it quite amusing. When she finally reached the inner circle she saw a face, one she had never seen before. "Who is she?"

"Jenni Porter," shouted a voice from the crowd.

"What happened to her?"

"Looks like she got hit by lightning," the voice came again.

"Better call 911."

The witches sneered from behind their hiding place in the trees that lined the streets.

"Excellent work, Sister," Sara retorted.

"But why did you kill her?" Melanie asked.

Nannette laughed with a chuckle that sounded more like a whisper. "It matters not who falls along the way. Just as rain falls on the wheat and the tares, so does lightning. Bad things *do* happen to good people."

"I thought you were just angry," the other two applauded.

Nannette turned to her sisters, her eyes burning, "I am."

Another flash struck another person in the crowded streets; the club hoppers scattered with screams of instant terror.

"We'd better get inside!" Dominique yelled, trying to get the attention of the panicked crowd. None listened; they just fled in every direction.

Melanie blinked, causing another surge to strike an onlooker. "That *does* make you feel better," she cackled.

"Ooh, ooh, my turn," Sara cried, focusing her attention on a teenager who was running toward them. She blinked, and the teen fell. "This is fun."

The witches all smiled, the moonlight glinting off their rotting teeth. "That one was a vampire, dear," Melanie grinned.

"Perhaps that will anger Set against us," Nannette

whined.

"Pity."

***

"You wanted to see me, Father?" Cassi said, entering Set's cavern. Set turned. His hooded cloak covered his features, engulfed his face. It seemed that as his power grew, the shadows embraced him more and more. Cassi stared into the faceless hood of his cloak.

He touched her face, his long nails tenderly crossing her cheek. She could feel their sharpness, even though his touch was light. "You *are* magnificent," he said, his voice rough and multiplied. "I am looking forward to your upcoming marriage. You are very special, my dear. My son would only choose to marry a princess. I know what he sees in you now, a power so dark and evil that it will bring the end to all good."

Cassi knew he was exaggerating. She could never be *that* evil, but his kind words meant much to her.

"Do you know what impresses me most?" Set asked.

Cassi paused, almost fearful of the answer. "I'm afraid not, Dark One."

"Ah, but you just spoke it. What impresses me most is that you still have incredible warmth around you. Normally a vampire submits to me within the first week of being transformed, yet somehow you defy me and cling to your light. I see you now, standing there, radiating more deadly heat than these pillars of fire," Set continued, touching the flames, turning them a ghostly

177

purple. "Almost godlike. You are 'afraid not.' Are you even afraid of me?"

"No," Cassi answered, her voice shaking.

Set snickered. "I already knew that, Child. I wanted to see you only to ask you this: Why have you not yet accepted the marriage proposal from my son? Is he not all you ever hoped for?"

"He is."

"I am prepared to give you my life, give you my son. All that the world holds for me is through him, and I give him to you. Why do you deny?"

Cassi shrunk, unsure. "I don't know. I mean, I know my life is yours forever; that is the way of things. There is no possible way to go back, is there? It puzzles even me. You see, I cannot see myself like *this* forever, but I feel as though the choice isn't mine."

"If you accept the proposal, the choice will be yours. You can take your life into your hands and squeeze it until it gives you the blood you deserve, the blood you yearn for."

"I want no part of blood," Cassi quivered. "You sound nervous, unsure of yourself, Father. Why?"

"It does not concern you."

"Then why bring up my future? Won't I have forever to decide to marry your son?"

"I would prefer that you didn't!"

Cassi balked, "What?"

Set turned quickly toward her, his arm flying, catching her cheek, and causing blood to run from the wound. "We are finished."

Cassi was shocked, but refused to back down. "Is

there a way for me to go back?"

Suddenly she knew she shouldn't have asked. Set pulled his cloak from his face, the shadows fleeing, revealing the maggots that tugged at his flesh. His eyes burned with incredible fury. "Just one," he stammered, raising a wooden stake.

A blast of light caught Set, sending him into the air. He landed with a harsh thud. Cassi saw the shadows creeping toward him, as if to make sure he was all right. The witches stood magnificently and proudly in the doorway. "Go," they whispered in unison.

Cassi didn't hesitate, just fled toward the door.

The witches approached Set, who was now groaning, rolling over. The sisters surrounded him. "Are you prepared to destroy all we have worked for? Slaying one of your own would cause your destruction and the destruction of evil, including your son. Are you willing to sacrifice all we have worked for because one of your children has not given herself fully to you? Then you are a fool, for we are winning, and the hour is at hand when *we* will ascend into glory."

Set stood, his face twisted in anger, but unable to destroy the three powers that now loomed above him.

"You are correct, *I* soon will be ascending in glory," Set barked. "Thank you for reminding me of our purpose. It will not happen again."

"No it shall not," the three whispered. They took one another's hands and glared together at Set.

His face was even more distorted with terror and anger. "You do not understand!"

"We will."

"No!"

But it was too late. The three witches blinked; Set's flesh contorted. His eyes grew wide as an extreme pressure tugged at his head. Darkness fell upon him that engulfed him painfully. The maggots burst, leaving their entrails upon Set's face. With a great scream of pain from an unbearable pressure, Set's flesh tore, ripping his head from his body. With an explosion, the fetid remains of the Dark Lord turned to dust.

The explosion was so intense that the wall directly behind where Set had stood now reflected the calm witches' reflections. Diamond had formed on the surface of the cavern wall.

In this moment Lucas entered the cavern, his alarmed face reflecting in the diamond. "Why?" he asked calmly, though his face flickered with obvious anger.

The witches turned to him. "He was going to destroy your bride, Lucas. She defied him as no one ever has before. She refused to give herself fully to him," they answered in unison, nodding in Cassi's direction when she entered the room.

Lucas turned to her, his eyes darting in a bewildered frenzy. "Is this true?"

"He raised a stake to me, Lucas. They truly saved my life."

Lucas's expression calmed. "Who will reign now?" he asked, hanging his head slightly.

Cassi took Lucas's arm and folded it over her own. "You will."

"I can't," Lucas said. "I don't have an heir."

"You will soon," the witches applauded. "Until then, we shall reign."

"With Melanie at the head," Nannette cried, "and I as her heir."

"And with I as Nannette's," Sara finished.

Melanie approached Lucas and Cassi. "You will take your proper place on your wedding night, Lucas, for on that night, Cassi shall conceive, and you will have an heir."

"Cassi has informed me that the engagement is off for now," Lucas retorted softly.

Melanie's face twisted at the news. "Why, child?" she spoke to Cassi.

"I cannot be with him forever, not yet."

"You still have not given yourself fully to your desires, your potential, your evil," Melanie said.

"It cannot be helped," Lucas stated sorrowfully.

"That it can," Melanie contradicted. Then, turning to Cassi, she clapped three times, and a large heavy book fell from the air into Melanie's gnarled hands. She flipped through the book. "We took away your choice once, we can do it again. *Desle Grate, rue en ester et intervolium!*"

Cassi felt a creeping cold inside of her that started at her feet and worked its way slowly up her body, throwing her into a fit of pain. She fell to the ground instantly and began writhing and twisting. Lucas watched, knowing what the spell would do for him, for her, and for his prosperity. He thought it strange that he hated to see Cassi in such pain. Finally the cold took refuge inside Cassi's heart, and with only vague recollections of her brief agony, she stood.

She was still herself, choice-making and free, but the nagging voices in her head were silent, and for the first time in Cassi's life, she could imagine her wedding day.

CHAPTER SIXTEEN

Time drifted like a dream on silky waves, crashing into crystal beaches. James and Rick sat pondering the difficult tasks that were unfolding before them. James had never seen the Protector so confused, so unsure of himself, and for a moment, he seemed practically mortal. James could tell that the last few days had taken their toll on the Protector, both emotionally and physically. The young skin that framed his face now was beginning to sag, and dark circles formed cool puddles under his eyes. He appeared old and tired. James imagined that he, himself, probably looked the same way. So they sat quietly in the grass, surrounded by the forest, trying to calm their screaming inner thoughts and emotions. The air was heavy, full of humidity for such an arid environment. Rick closed his eyes and breathed fully through his mouth, the air escaping with a rushing force that James heard like a wind dancing in the trees.

"What time is it?" James finally asked, breaking the silence and hoping for a nap.

"Just past six in the morning, it seems," Rick answered.

James stared into the stars above him, watching the sun begin to peek from behind the mountains. It refused to paint the sky with its colors, but James was satisfied, for the sun was again rising from the east. "We must have done something right to correct the balance of the world," he beamed.

"If only it were that easy," the Protector answered. As he spoke, James noticed another great disturbance. The sun had begun to rise, but now was falling, recoiling back into the shadows. In moments, the sun had vanished, again abandoning the world to darkness.

A look that resembled fear and disgust crossed James's face. "What does that mean?" he asked.

The Protector answered in almost a whisper, "*His coming will mark the hold of black roots; its disease will spread to new heights of the sky...*"

"What?"

"A greater evil, more evil than Set, now rules the shadows," Rick said, still barely audible, looking like he was more interested in telling himself this information than he was in telling it to James. "Set has been overthrown. The witches now rule, and they *again* meddle in fate. Her choice is no longer her own. No. She thinks it is still her own. She believes she has the will to choose. Then does she or doesn't she? *A cackle of chaos.*"

He stood and began to pace, not listening to or

seeing anything but his own thoughts. "The sign in the sky," he repeated. Then his glazed look cleared instantly as his eyes narrowed and burrowed deeply into James's. "Three days of darkness mark the nights before the final battle, but it wasn't supposed to happen this soon. So, thanks to our dear slayer who freely speeds up fate, it is much nearer now. Yes. Come James, we have much to prepare, for there can be no darkness except in the absence of light."

***

The day rolled on in darkness when there should have been light. The stars twinkled in the heavens, casting awkward silvery shadows across the world. Lucas took Cassi's hand. They sprawled out across the grass, letting its natural coolness envelop them.

"The sky is beautiful," Lucas said.

Cassi was scanning the stars. "It is almost perfect. Everything is so bright."

"I love this," Lucas continued. "Us, life, *we* are almost perfect."

"Almost?" Cassi whispered.

Lucas paused and turned to look at her. "Marry me."

Cassi laughed softly, "I'm planning to."

"No," Lucas said, "marry me tomorrow."

Cassi couldn't help but laugh again. "Tomorrow? Now why would you want to get married tomorrow?"

"Why not?" Lucas asked. "After all, the sooner we get married, the sooner I take my place as Lord of Evil, and the sooner you become queen. The sooner we have children. The sooner... please, now, start your life with me... tomorrow."

There was a tone of seriousness in his voice that Cassi couldn't brush off. She felt heat between them. She knew that she loved him, and he loved her. It wasn't just a game for her. It couldn't be a game for him. There was no question about it. She turned and caught his eyes, which had grown large, like those of a puppy that was about to come home to its owner for the first time. Lucas touched her cheek, a touch that felt so right, so good that it sent energy coursing through her as nothing ever had. Warmth came to her, wrapping her in an inexpressible feeling. "Yes," she finally answered. "Yes."

***

Rick and James stepped quietly into the almost desolate library, ignoring the librarian's suspicious glare. They coursed through the aisles, skimming pages of novels, books, and encyclopedias dealing with witchcraft, Egyptian myth, or any mystical entity.

"What are we looking for?" James asked. "And why are people working today? Don't they get that something is up?"

"I'll know when I find it," Rick answered, flipping quickly through the pages of *Mythological Vampires*. "Humans tend to ignore things they can't explain. It is better to not deal with the unknown. People think that asking questions can only harm them, so they go on with everyday life as if nothing is the matter."

"Doesn't *Amun-Ra* hold the answer?" James asked. "To whatever we are looking for."

"*Amun-Ra* holds the prophecies of the future; we are looking to defeat the present." He slapped the book closed, rubbing his eyes. "This is worthless; there is nothing here."

James looked bewildered, almost angry. How did the Protector know there was nothing for them when they had only been looking for twenty minutes? Rick ducked into an aisle that was filled with shadows.

James followed, perturbed. He squinted in reaction to a blinding flash as he rounded the corner and saw Rick reach into the bookshelf. No, he was reaching into a book. James saw the shelf quiver, and in a moment, a door swung open.

"Are you coming?" Rick asked.

James closed his eyes, took a breath, and stepped through the doorway. As he crossed the threshold, he noticed an unexpected thickness in the air. His skin felt like it was stretching, and an incredible force sucked him through the door. When he opened his eyes, he was standing in a large, circular room, with marble floors and books that lined the walls. A bright light emanated from an unknown source. "Where are we?" James asked.

"A library open only to the Powers That Be," Rick answered, walking directly to a wall of books that seemed magically suspended in midair. Rick pulled a book entitled *Fate and Forces* off the shelf. He smiled when the pages fell open clumsily. "I figured."

"What?" James asked.

"Fate hasn't written whether good or evil is going to win yet, meaning that we still have a chance at victory."

"I thought you knew what fate was doing," James said.

"It has been hiding things from me ever since I interfered. They won't allow me to meddle again. Therefore, we have to find someone else to get in the middle of the situation."

James snorted with a smile on his face. "Fate isn't sentient; it can't make decisions. Only the Powers That Be can decide."

Now Rick smiled, continuing to thumb through the pages of the book. "That, my friend, is where you are only partially correct. You see, fate is more than just what is going to happen to a specific individual in a given amount of time. It is a great scale, balancing the powers of the world. It creates the Powers That Be in order to carry out its desires and wishes. But, the Powers That Be are more; they control fate by limiting their own actions. So it is a great tug-of-war, a constant pulling of the universe in several directions. At first glance, it seems that fate has decided a terrible fortune to fall upon this world. The only reason it would cause such distress is if the Powers That Be got bored or tired, if they were unwilling to continue to write the stories of people's lives; but this book tells me differently."

"Why do the Powers That Be have a library anyway?" James questioned. "I'm sure they don't have much time for reading."

Rick's smile burst into a grin. "The library is a recordkeeping place filled with the decisions of every human being in this world. Fate writes the books to keep record, so it does not forget what it has planned for the future or already carried out in the past, and so that it can judge human beings for what they have done. This book is the newest volume and should be filled with the future knowledge that I would have already been familiar with, had it not been for the Powers That Be attempting to contradict fate in its never-ending struggle."

"You know everything in every one of these books?"

"Yes and no. I have access to the information, all of it. Yet I know only when it becomes expedient for me to know."

"So we broke into a library that holds the secrets to the future. Wonderful," James trailed off, browsing the aisles himself. "We'd better not get caught. I'd bet that is punishable by more than thirty days of community service. So what does it say?"

Rick's eyes scanned the pages.

James couldn't read his expression.

Rick spoke softly, "There is someone who knows. Someone who *has* had the end revealed to him."

"Who?"

"My mother is quite an amazing woman, James. She is a great interferer when she knows her son cannot do so himself. I must speak with…"

"Your mother? Is she the one who knows?"

"No…"

"Why would the Powers That Be hide it from you?" James asked.

"I know what I must," the Protector said slapping the book shut quickly, ignoring James's questions. "I will be gone the rest of the day; please be careful in my absence."

"Where are you going?"

"Purgatory, to speak to the person that knows."

And in a whisper of light, the Protector vanished.

CHAPTER SEVENTEEN

The pristine sands of the Sahara Desert stretched on through the infinite horizon as the scorching sun beat down upon it. High above the dunes in the clean Libyan air, where only wisps of clouds danced along a sapphire sky, flew a dark falcon. Its magnified shadow skidded across the sand as the cool upper air rustled through its feathers.

The falcon stiffened his wings, fanned his tail, twisted his body, and began a dive toward the sand. His razor claws were pulled tightly against his body until he was ready to stretch them outward and...

He never pulled up.

There was a thump as sand was thrown into the air, and Horus began walking along the dunes. Hot air swirled around him, throwing sand into his naked eyes. He sunk with every step, the loose sand giving way to his weight. Footsteps were rarely seen here, deep in the heart of the desert, amongst the towering dunes.

The dry air and late afternoon sun evaporated the sweat from Horus's bare arms and dried his throat as he breathed. He felt his lungs grow tight in the parched air, surprised at how quickly he grew thirsty. This was his first visit to the desert as a mortal—really his first visit in over a century.

Eventually he fell on his face in the sand, overcome by thirst.

"I saw you fly in, Horus, and have no doubt the Powers That Be left you with your ability to control your own death," a voice echoed.

Horus grinned and rolled onto his back, "Well, As, I just wanted to see if your heart for helping those perishing in the desert was still as strong as it used to be. At least help me up."

A being with the muscular body of a man and the head of a hawk reached down with a strong arm and lifted Horus to his feet. "It is good to see you again. Ever since Set was banished to the underworld, the deserts have been calm."

"So then, you don't miss your old friend Set?" Horus asked.

"Not since he turned."

"Ah. Well if you are on my side, then how about some water?"

As spread his beak and made a sound resembling laughter. "The desert is a strange place to most, but a beloved one to me. People flock to the beaches, with their white stretching sands. I really don't understand why they don't like the desert."

"Probably because there is no *water*," Horus jested.

"Maybe you just don't know where to look."

A low rumble shook the sand as the dunes fell flat, revealing large palm trees and rocky cliffs. A shimmering fall of blue water poured over smooth ledges into a rippling pool. Beautiful pink and orange flowers sprouted from the sand and reached toward the sun as Horus and As became surrounded by a previously invisible oasis.

"So this is the treatment for those who become lost in your desert," Horus said, admiring the shade and cool breeze that skidded across the pool's surface. "You obviously have not lost your touch."

As nodded his head in a sort of bow. "What brings you to my solitude, Son of Osiris?"

Horus helped himself to a handful of water from the pool. "Actually, I need you to bring me a river of water, one that leads to the underworld."

"Ah, well, we must wait for Ra to bring the sun, for the river I cannot bring until the sun comes low enough to touch my desert."

"It already grows large in the horizon. We will wait in your oasis until we can summon the river."

"Going to visit your father, Horus?"

"Unfortunately, no. I imagine I will see him, but I have business with Set."

As looked surprised, but said nothing. His black eyes remained emotionless as he watched the large sun stain the sky pink. "I believe Ra is with you this night. He sets the sun down much more quickly for your sake. He will soon have to pass through the gates to the underworld. They will be preparing to receive him. I believe we can try to summon your river now."

"Thank you, As."

With another rumble, As became lost in concentration; the cliff that spilled the water into the pool became deep and hollow. It grew black, like a monstrous doorway as the pool of water was consumed in its depths. Horus watched as the cave in the cliff grew wider and darker. The sun grew near, and the cave engulfed it. Two lions guarded the entrance to the cave, one facing east, and the other, west.

Horus advanced confidently. The lions roared as he approached the large bars sealing the entrance to the cavern.

"I must pass, Aker, guardian of the underworld."

"Why, Horus!" the lions roared with a hint of surprise. "I hear you've been gallivanting around as a mortal. About time you came to reclaim your roots."

"It is that 'gallivanting around as a mortal' that brings me here tonight. I have business in the underworld."

"Never can finish anything without daddy, can you?"

"Just open the gate."

"Are you sure you are pure enough to enter? You may become trapped if Anubis finds you unworthy."

"I am your master, and your lord. I will take the risk. Open the gate."

"As you desire."

The heavy gate screeched open. Horus ducked behind the two opposing lions and passed into the cavern. It smelled deep and damp here, and the rocky terrain blocked the light of the stars. Horus's body glowed, however, providing him with enough light to see. A dark river ran like blood in the darkness; Horus could hear it rushing rapidly toward the underworld. In the darkness he could see a small, gondola-like boat approaching, meandering through the water. As it drew closer, two people took shape in the darkness, one lying comfortably at the bow, while another, standing in the back, steered the boat with a giant wooden pole. The boat glided slowly to a stop on the bank where Horus stood.

"Hello again, Aken. Aken? Oh, Mahaf. Aken seems to be sleeping again," Horus called out.

"Well hello, Horus. Seems I have to be waking him more and more often. He's pretty peaceful when a celestial being wants to be picked up."

Horus chuckled. "Same old Aken, I suppose."

Mahaf stretched his pole out toward the sleeping god and pushed him into the water. Horus heard a splash, followed by a gasp, but after only a moment, Aken stood on the deck of the small ferry, dripping wet.

"Thanks, Mahaf," he said.

"No problem, sir."

"Horus! It is great to see you. Come on aboard."

"You too, Aken. I trust all is well?"

"All is as it should be, Horus. Come, come now, and let's get you across."

Horus stepped up on the gondola, and as he sat down, Mahaf pushed his pole into the river and back into the current. The boat rocked slightly as it sped along twists and turns beneath the Earth. Mahaf had navigated these rivers an infinite number of times, and he turned along branches, avoided waterfalls, and pushed the boat along in the dark almost effortlessly. Aken immediately took his spot at the bow of the ship, propped up one leg, and began snoring within minutes.

"It was interesting," Mahaf started, "bringing Set here. I always figured it would be you to kill him."

"I'm not sure I could ever stoop to his level," Horus responded. "My mother always taught me to be a lover of light. Well… at least I always believed she would have taught me that if she had the chance to raise me."

"She hid you well, for a purpose: to undo the evil that Set brought upon your family."

"Yes, and now an evil greater than he has destroyed him. I never thought I would personally kill him, but I had hoped one of my slayers would. They are so talented."

"That Cynthia of yours *was* amazing. I don't think I'll ever forget her. When Anubis weighed her heart against the feather, her heart was so light she immediately went to paradise. I don't think she could have ever thought badly about someone. She spoke nothing but greatness about you."

"She knew she would die, and still she fought with courage and conviction."

"I think all slayers know they are going to die. Not many last very long."

"Which is unfortunate," Horus said, bowing his head a little. "What a great calling, but for many, their joy on Earth is not yet full when they die."

"Have *you* forgotten the bigger picture, my friend? Earth is such a small piece. Seconds or years in a lifetime mean nothing compared to eternity. Cynthia was not disappointed to leave. Apprehensive, perhaps. Not disappointed."

The boat veered to the right and rounded a corner. As it did, the cavern filled with light. Mahaf pushed the ferry into a magnificent lagoon with torches that lined the walls and glistened off the calm water. People were lined up on shore, on what looked like a great platform with steps leading up from the water. The ground shimmered like gold, and the people were all dressed in blissful white.

"We're here," Mahaf said dispassionately, pulling up sideways to the land. Horus stepped from the gondola and was immediately met by Aken's wife, Ament.

"Welcome to the land of the dead," she said with a warm smile. "It's nice to meet you... eh..."

"Relax, Ament. It's Horus, and he's not dead," Aken yawned from the boat.

"Horus? Oh my! I didn't recognize you. You look so... mortal."

He laughed, "Yes, yes, my clothes, I know. I can never please anyone with them. I'll tell you though, after this journey, I have been looking forward to your bread."

Ament looked pleased. With Horus in stride beside her, she walked over to a small table with bread and a large, clear pitcher of water. With motherly care she sliced a piece off a large loaf, buttered it gently, and handed it to Horus, who took it eagerly.

"It's still warm."

"Just out of the fires," Ament said, pouring a cup from the pitcher.

"You never cease to amaze me. How do you make bread so mouth-watering?" Horus took the cup of water from Ament's outstretched hand and pressed it to his parched mouth.

"The flour of the gods, I suppose," Ament joked charmingly. After a moment of silence she continued, "I know we can't keep you for long. I'm sure you have work to attend to. You know where to go, just through that gate," she said, motioning behind her to an ominous wooden door with no handle. "You'll have to knock hard, since no one is expecting you."

Horus's chewing slowed. "Are you expecting someone tonight?" he asked, suddenly realizing that the warm bread was not meant especially for him.

"We're not sure," came the response, Ament not meeting his eyes. Then she added a bit too quickly, "Well... off you go."

Horus handed the cup back to Ament, thanked her with a kiss on her hand, and proceeded toward the back of the cavern, toward the looming wooden door. His knock echoed through the hall, and the door creaked open on old hinges. Horus entered a small room, with only a table in one corner and a giant scale pushed back into the wall. This was his least favorite part.

He felt trapped, as if in an examination chamber, when he climbed onto the table and sat annoyed, waiting for the next part of his journey to be completed. The room was lit by a single torch on the wall, making the space dark and foreboding. Horus was sure this was Set's favorite part of the expedition.

Then a large, black shadow stretched from the wall, devouring what little light was cast onto the floor. It reached toward Horus with unseen hands, twisting its way to the god of light. The shadow began to take shape, the head first, of a jackal, but black. Yellow eyes surveyed him, and soon, a full-sized man stood in the room.

"Let's get this over with, Anubis," Horus demanded. "You know this is my least favorite part."

Anubis's only response was a malevolent grin.

A door in the rock swung open harshly, and a woman came in, carefully holding a feather balanced on a pillow. "Oh," she exclaimed at her father's unpleasant face. "Dad, stop trying to scare the poor patient!" Then she turned to address Horus. "Don't worry about him; he's a lot more bark than he is bite... Oh!" she exclaimed as she caught Horus's eye. "Horus, it's you!"

"Hello, Kabechet."

"Why, oh my! Can I bring you something to drink?"

"No thank you, Kabechet. Ament took care of me earlier. Besides, Anubis here doesn't have an entire embalming to do. Just a weighing, I suppose."

Anubis gestured to the scale in the room.

Horus rolled his eyes, got off the table, and stepped up on one side of the rusted scale. He watched the needle tip toward him, crossed his arms, and said, "I still don't understand how this thing is only supposed to weigh my heart."

Anubis said nothing, just took the feather from off

the pillow, and gently laid it opposite Horus on the scale.

Horus rose a little, but not as much as he knew he should have.

"Your heart is heavy," Kabechet stated wide-eyed. "Heavier than the feather!"

"Impossible," Horus protested.

"Horus, with a heavy heart you are never going to make it back to the surface; no one ever has!"

Horus snorted and pushed off the scale. "I insist you let me see my father, so that I can get his permission to speak with Set."

Anubis just pointed toward a stone doorway, hidden in the rock.

"Good day, Horus," Kabechet chimed.

But her words, *you are never going to make it back,* hung in his mind. He knew why he had a heavy heart.

"Are you in love, my son?" a voice echoed through a copper-colored cavern. Huge stalactites stretched down toward the ground, dripping slowly with the water that gradually added to their strength.

Horus looked up to see a large granite throne far at the end of a great hall. To his sides were doorways, each marked with a hieroglyph. Horus knew where some of the doors led, but he hoped he would never have to find out about the others.

At the feet of the man who sat on the large throne laid a beast, a demon with the head of a crocodile, the torso of a leopard, and the hindquarters of a hippopotamus. The crocodile head seemed to smile sinisterly at Horus through sharp teeth, although he was still too far away to tell.

Horus's footsteps echoed heavily through the hall. His rhythm kept time with his beating heart. "No, Father, to love is against my rules."

Osiris moved his hand from the armrest of the stone throne and held his chin with it pensively. "Anubis told me you failed your test. Your heart is heavy. You won't make it out of the underworld with a heavy heart. I trust you will resolve the issue quickly, so that you may get back to your task in the world of the living."

"Yes, Father."

The beast at the foot of Osiris made a sound resembling a deep-throated growl. In a flash she opened her powerful jaws and headed for Horus. He winced at the thought of her razor-sharp teeth burying into his still living flesh. She was Ammit, devourer of the wicked, of those whose hearts were heavy, but Horus wasn't dead yet!

With a snap of great power, Osiris pulled on a leash that had appeared around her neck. Strong chains restrained the beast mere moments before her teeth would have pierced Horus's skin.

Horus let out his breath, never remembering the moment he inhaled deeply to hold it.

"Ammit senses your weakness," Osiris stated coolly.

"Yes, Father. I am here to speak with Set, that I may resolve the matter."

"Would it resolve the matter?" Osiris questioned.

"Why is it, Father, that you insist on being so formal with me when this is a matter that does not concern you? Let me speak to Set that I may resolve this matter and return to those who care about me."

"Why is it that children think they know everything?" Osiris asked to the stillness of the room. "Go if you must, my son, but do not take me for a fool. I know the desires of your heart, and I fail to see how you are going to resolve your problems by speaking with Set. Shouldn't you take it up with the person it concerns?"

Horus looked cross. "I'll need to get out of here in order to do that, won't I?"

"Then you are in quite the predicament, for you will not be able to return to the world of the living with a heart that wishes to be dead, and since you cannot resolve your issue in the world of the dead, you must return to the world of the living. You've gotten yourself into a paradoxical situation this time, my son."

"I'll figure a way. Now through which door do I need to pass to find Set?"

"The one with his symbol, of course."

Horus turned his back to his father and began searching doors. When he found the one with the hieroglyph of a black pig, he paced toward that door.

"Horus."

He turned.

"I want to let you know that I'm proud of you. You worked hard to avenge my death."

A single tear fell from Horus's eye before he regained his composure. "There is still work to be done."

"Yes, well, don't be a stranger."

Horus put his hand to the door, pushed, and entered the place where the wicked await judgment.

CHAPTER EIGHTEEN

After Rick had left the library, James took to one of the comfortable, overstuffed chairs that were tucked behind a bookshelf in the far corner of the building. He had browsed the rows of books and found himself excited to read on the very subject that had been troubling him: how to tell whether a spell was originating from a source that was good or evil. He could feel, in the air perhaps, when something was brewing, but whether that spell was cast by a fellow warlock trying to do something good for the world, or by someone who had darker intentions, he couldn't determine. He felt that way tonight: an emotion that churned his stomach, yet made his head feel light and joyful.

So he curled up in the soft chair and began reading:

Power is a real thing, and the discernment of

such is a gift equal to that of discerning a spirit—it is a gift that one must earn. How is it that you can tell whether a "feeling" comes from God or yourself, Satan or yourself, or one of the many other voices of Fate and Destiny? Do you receive answers to prayers because you willed it so? Discernment comes down to readiness and the worthiness of the questioner to receive an answer. It is the same when force is felt. Some, being more practiced, seasoned, or prepared, can automatically discover the source of a power, while others may need to first have a more enlightened understanding of the many sources of energy acting upon the earth.

James's eyes became heavy as he read on: "Try to use your intuition—your right to power—as you read this book, for it has been enchanted to teach you, depending on your already achieved level of power."

He was no longer reading, the book was speaking to him, "It was written for you, James, to show you what evil feels like, that you may recognize it more fully, since you already know what good is like."

"No!"

James's eyes snapped open to the sound of this bloodcurdling scream:

"No! You Satanist! You can't!"

At first, James was disoriented, but as he looked toward the screams, his head cleared.

"My son! My child! No!"

The cries came from a woman, a beautiful woman, who was restrained on an altar, held down by six beasts.

James recognized them immediately as vampires, but they looked different somehow—ancient.

"Set! I will have my revenge! First you kill my husband, exile my Horus, take me by force to be your wife, and now you carry off my baby! Why do you stand there? Why torment me longer?"

James realized she was screaming at him, with a fire in her eyes unlike any he had ever seen. He looked down at a crying baby in his arms. Suddenly he understood: he was Set. He knew where he was—a pyramid, built by his followers: vampires, and those who worshipped them.

He turned to leave, the screams echoing in his ears, littered with profanities and the pleas of this desecrated mother.

"I will kill Judas for the awful pain he has wrought in my heart and for the evil he has placed in yours! And I will hide my Horus until he grows to power, and it shall be he who takes his revenge on you! Monster! Fiend! Creature of hell! Bring him back! Lucas! Your mother loves you!" she cried.

Set could hear her wailings until he had left the pyramid. As he did, he looked down at the child and smiled.

***

"Sir? Sir! The library is closing."

James woke with a shudder. He was drenched in sweat, a pit in his stomach.

"You fell asleep, sir," the librarian stated. "You

must have been having a bad dream." She glanced down at the book that was lying in his lap. "Perhaps you should try something a little more uplifting before you go to sleep. I'd suggest the Bible," she stated with a judgmental look in her eye. After she was satisfied that he understood the look, she repeated, "We're closing now."

James couldn't say anything; a feeling of horror filled his whole body. He wiped the sweat off his forehead with his sleeve, stood, and walked toward the door without realizing that he had let the book fall to the floor. The cool mountain air felt good on his hot skin. All he could think about was the evil figure that he was in that dream. It consumed him. He had never felt so dark.

It was then that he realized he had been feeling this way all day. Now it was clear to him; the feeling of power that he didn't know—didn't know if it was good or evil, light or dark. He knew now. Why? Because he knew what evil felt like. He had become evil in that dream. It was pure evil that permeated the air. It had a stench. He could smell it now. He could hear the screams of the just crying out to him to seek revenge against the power. He had to silence it, had to know its source. He set off looking for it in the night.

He followed his gut. He could feel the evil growing with every step he took until it led him to the three witch sisters.

They stood in a silent circle, hand in hand, enjoying the rain and lightning that flashed in mystical formations around them. The place in which they stood was familiar; they were standing in the same grassy clearing they had stood in the night Cassi had begun her new life. The clearing was different now, darker even than it had ever been before. Each sister stood, eyes closed, basking in her work and the darkness she had successfully brought into the world. The wind whipped their hair across their faces, stinging with the pleasure of pain. Their robes flew violently about their feet, slapping the wet grass, and more lightning struck above them than anywhere else in the valley.

"The night is falling. The wedding comes," Sara spoke, breaking the silence.

"Your ruling hand comes to a close," Nannette spoke to Melanie.

"When Lucas's child is born he shall reign even greater than I, and we will be powerful servants ready to assist him in his glory," Melanie continued.

"And we shall assist in releasing the power of purgatory upon this pitiful world!" Sara exclaimed.

The sisters laughed, a cackle that rose to heaven, making it tremble. Lightning darted in all directions.

"Wait!" Melanie cried, raising her hand in a manner of power. The world fell silent; the witches obeyed her command. "Someone is watching from the forest. There."

She whirled and caught the brown eyes of someone in the trees. "You!" she cried. "Do not try to run; your legs are useless! Come to meet us, since you insist on watching us."

James glided out of his hiding space in the trees, his heart fearful; he was powerless to stop his progression toward the sisters.

Nannette smiled. "A mortal? But you have the potential to have such great power."

James felt like he was being pulled from the inside, as if a fishhook was ripping his stomach. Only his toes could touch the ground as his bloodshot eyes drifted to where the witches stood. The pain ended when his feet finally supported his weight, face to face and just inches from Melanie's icy eyes.

"We are the same, you and I," Melanie stated coldly. "We both have the potential for great things. We are kinsfolk, because we are both witches, powerful and evil."

"I am not like you," James finally said, gathering courage.

"Aren't you?" Melanie asked, her hand bursting into flames, the fire gliding like water over her flesh. "You remember this trick, do you not?"

"Your power comes from the Devil; mine does not."

Melanie sneered. "You are correct." She paused. "Your power… comes from *me*."

"What?"

"Welcome home, Son."

James laughed. "How dare you? My mother was killed when I was born. She gave her life to bring me into this world. How dare you defile her memory."

"How can I defile a memory of a mother whose face you cannot remember? Your father's name was William. He was a master of the dark arts. We met in July, eighteen years ago. He promised to take care of you until this day, when I was to take you and train you to become who you were meant to be. Then, he was murdered, the person who killed him never found. The only clues to his death were two puncture wounds to his neck."

"Your knowledge of how my father died proves nothing. I know the shadows can whisper secrets to you. It is no secret to the deepest shadows of purgatory how my father died."

Melanie chuckled. "Those shadows whisper to you too, and one is whispering to you now. What is it saying? Ah yes, he isn't dead!"

Melanie turned and took the hands of the other witches. A sparking column of blackness rose from the center of their circle, and in moments, James's father stood amidst the sisters. His eyes were yellow, his face twisted, but James recognized him immediately. "We've been together all this time," Melanie whispered.

James felt a rising revulsion.

"You are only half mortal, Son," Melanie said. "Only half Tongan really. The other half... is me."

James's mind was whirling. He hadn't seen his father in over five years. It was his father who began to teach him the mysteries of witchcraft. When his father died, James found his spell books. Were they placed there purposely for James to find, so that he would study the craft? Was this witch really his lost mother, who he had thought was so noble for giving her life in sacrifice for his? It all seemed impossible, but James understood his life now: the strange circumstances surrounding his mother's death, the absence of her death certificate and gravestone, his father's reluctance to discuss or help him search for information on his mother. Then his father had disappeared on a fishing trip with a friend who would only come around at night, and was also later proclaimed dead. James never thought about the strange friend, but now knew exactly who, or what, that friend was. James now clearly remembered feeling a heavy dread when the friend arrived at his father's doorstep… when *Set* arrived at his father's doorstep.

James's mind was fuzzy as Melanie approached to hug him. "You know you don't fit in here," she said. "You are unlike all of the others. You are looked down upon because of your gifts. Intolerance courses through this town as surely as blood courses through your veins. Just look at the death of that slayer. The town didn't investigate as it should have. She was different too. You are different in more ways than one. There is only one way to stop the prejudice. You must leave. You must become what you were born to become. Leave the life that betrays you. Leave the people who claim to be your friends, who claim to want to help you but don't understand *how* to help you. We are your family. We understand your needs and desires, and we will help you bring them to pass."

She stepped back, and James's father approached, arms outstretched. "You'll join us now, of course," his father said, embracing him. In James's mind, the embrace lasted too long. Then he understood why. "This won't hurt," his father intoned.

"No," James whispered. "Please don't."

James then heard a low growl and felt cold breath on his neck. James released his embrace and pulled out a wooden stake he had tucked into his belt. When he released his grip on the stake, it hung magically suspended in the air. James hesitated momentarily, as he reconsidered; then, the stake, taking a life of its own, plummeted quickly into the back of James's father, piercing his heart. James pushed his father away, noticing with anguish and horror, the surprised look on his face before a faint popping sound filled the air with dust.

"That, *my child*, was a mistake," Melanie hissed angrily.

"Death is better than living with you," James said, his eyes narrowing.

Melanie raised her hands. "Then so be it!"

A trickle of sparks left her fingertips, moving slowly in a wave that rippled the air and sounded like thousands of bells echoing across a canyon. The wave moved slowly, its steady approach raising a torturous fear in its awaiting victim.

James was afraid and did the only thing he could think to do. His hands raised, he cried out, "*Protectamos.*"

Melanie cackled, "You think your insignificant power is any match for me?"

The sparks approached and struck around James with a sound like that of a sword clashing into a large metallic shield. James was thrown backward and slammed into the trunk of a tree, but he was alive. From the ground, he cried out, "Father taught me well, witch!"

"Your father was a fool."

The storm continued to pound the clearing with rain. Melanie looked up at the clouds, her eyes glowing solid white. James felt his hair standing on end, as the air around him filled with static. He rolled as lightning struck the tree he was under, shattering it to pieces, showering him with slivers of wood. When James looked at his mother, the anger was evident on her face.

"I am done playing games with you."

With that, she raised her hands again. The splinters of wood rose from the ground, aiming at James, encapsulating him in a cage of death.

"Make your peace with whatever God you believe in," Melanie rasped.

She clapped her hands, and the wood splinters shot toward James. "No!" he cried, extending his hands in front of him, attempting to block the blow. He prepared for the pain of his death, but it never came. James opened his eyes, and to his surprise, the wood splinters yielded to his command. He saw Melanie, struggling to maintain control of the entrapment. James could feel the weight of her power bearing down on him, but he pushed out with all his might, holding up a wall that was intently bearing down upon him.

Melanie's hands began to quiver; beads of sweat gathered on her brow. "You are no match for me, Child. Give up now!"

James noticed that he, too, was sweating, or was it the rain that was beating down on him? He couldn't tell, but he was determined. "I will hold out until you perish in a pile of your own vomit, you insignificant whore!"

Melanie narrowed her eyes. "You will die in the same way you destroyed your father. Come, sisters, give me your strength."

Nannette and Sara took Melanie's outstretched hands and with an evil glare flicked their wrists toward James.

The weight that he could previously barely withstand now tripled. James locked his elbows in hope that he could hold out, just a little longer. "Never, never, never," he whispered to himself. Then, following a loud snap, James looked down to see blood cascading down his arm. The pressure bearing down on him continued to increase; he was going to be crushed. Another snap and James had a moment to look, to see a white bone jutting violently from his arm. "No!" he screamed, as his arm collapsed into itself under the pressure, and thousands of wood splinters drove deeply into his heart.

CHAPTER NINETEEN

The boat rocked gently as Horus made his way back from the underworld. For the first time Horus could remember, Aken was wide-awake and stared at him peculiarly from the bow.

"What is it, Aken?"

Aken glanced downward momentarily, before meeting Horus's eyes. "Did you find out what you needed from Set?"

"Our conversation was sublime. Set said nothing to me, but the look in his eyes told me everything I needed to know."

"What did you see?"

"Hatred."

"And what did you ask of him?"

Horus's lips curved into a half smile. "I asked him why he attempted to kill the chosen one when she was his only hope of winning the war."

"And?"

"Well, dear Aken, I think I know how to bring our

suffering to an end."

Mahaf quit rowing in the middle of a wide space where the river flowed slowly. "We're here. This is where you need to get off."

"I know, Mahaf. I've done this before," Horus said, swinging his legs over the side of the boat and sliding gently into the calm waters.

"Wait," Aken blurted. "There's something else you need to know."

Horus turned, his wet hair sticking to his forehead. "What?"

Aken towered above him while standing on the ferry, but looked low and depressed. "We ferried someone across tonight."

Horus looked confused, "I thought you weren't expecting anyone."

"We can't tell him!" Mahaf whispered sternly.

"He should know before he goes back," Aken contended.

"Who?" Horus asked, the confusion twisting his face.

"We don't want to make your heart any heavier. You'll need to be light if you intend on getting out of here still... alive," Aken said, as if suddenly changing his mind, not willing to tell him.

"Who did you ferry to the underworld, Aken?" Horus demanded.

Aken paused before saying, "James."

Horus's heart sank.

"I'm sorry, Horus. I thought you should hear it from us."

Horus just nodded his head while treading water and began swimming away from the boat. James was dead, but... he couldn't think about it. Even now the water was moving more quickly, and Horus could hear the distinctive sound it made as it tumbled over a cliff in the distance. He had to be happy. He had to be light. He had to go upward, even though the water fell downward. He couldn't allow a thought for his friend; even a thought was too much.

The cliff approached.

He had to think of the good.

The water rushed toward it.

He had to think of fighting for light.

The roaring of the falls were upon him.

He had to finish what he started.

He plummeted over the edge.

***

When he woke up, he was in a bright white room lying on his stomach, face down, soaking wet.

"You didn't make it," a familiar voice said.

The light in the room was almost blinding as he rolled over and forced himself to make the blurry figure in front of him come into focus.

"I actually had to save *you*!" the voice echoed cheerfully.

"Cynthia?" Horus blinked, "but you're... you're..."

"Dead? Yes, but as Aken told you, I went to paradise rather quickly, and now, well, now I'm an angel... of sorts."

"You're an archangel? Servant to the Powers That Be?"

"Servant is such a degrading term. I prefer beautiful assistant."

Horus chuckled and steadied his spinning head.

"Actually, they need to see you," Cynthia said.

"And I them."

"Yes, of course. I'll leave you with each other then."

Horus stood and found himself surrounded by glinting walls, addressing a being that sat casually on a large golden throne.

The being glowed and emanated heat in the form of light. His skin was golden; he looked as though he were a moving monument, a statue of powerful universal forces.

"You hid it from me," the Protector said, not questioning.

"We did," the being spoke, his voice even more powerful than the Protector's.

"Why? Have I not been punished enough for my misdeeds? You took away the only person left on my side. If you take away my visions how do you expect me to continue to protect the world as I have been assigned?"

"The point of you living as a mortal was for you to learn to think, act, and be like them while maintaining your integrity. We cannot give you all of the answers. You must figure it out for yourself."

"Maintain my integrity while becoming a mortal? What juxtaposition! The prophecy says that one will make light prevail. How am I supposed to do that without any knowledge of future events, and with no help from any good *living* mortal? You stole my friend without explanation. Explain yourself! Why?"

The being paused, looking as though he was getting bored. After much thought he spoke, "Reconsider the prophecy. As for your 'friend,' he disrespected us. It isn't iniquity for *you* to read fate's books of life, but it becomes an issue when a mortal who has had so much written about him does."

"You took his life because he stood in the presence of your over-glorified library?"

"Fate didn't think it was a problem either. 'He didn't read anything,' fate said. Well it's too late now. It is time for fate to decide an ending. This world is getting so boring. Your friend is the only reason why it still exists! He sparked our interest when we realized how entertaining it would be for him to find out about his parents."

"You toy with the humans as if they are your game pieces," the Protector shouted.

"It would be a game if fate would stick its nose into someone else's business and leave us alone. This game would come to an end very quickly if it were up to me."

"Praise fate for its interference then."

"You snap at me, Protector, as if you know something I don't," the being said.

"I do know something you don't. You toy with me. You toy with the people down there, all for your own amusement. You send me down to live with them, be like them, to help *me*, you say? Yet I was denied the human experience. It was still against my rules to meddle, hate, cheat, lie, deceive, trust, distrust, and even love. How is that an education?"

"It—"

"That was a rhetorical question," the Protector interrupted. "I don't expect you to answer it."

"Do not be disrespectful to me, creature," the being spoke, angered, "or you will regret what you say."

"Don't threaten me! Fate decides who I am. You cannot change its course. Fate has given you the most basic of knowledge and your misinterpretation of that knowledge has the same potential danger of a child who wields his father's gun."

"Then it is time for that gun to fight back, and believe me, the gun will win, for it holds the bullets."

"A gun cannot fire itself. Or am I wrong? Have you, a Power That Is, decided an outcome for the upcoming battle? Is that your universal jurisdiction? No, I didn't think so."

"Fate knows all and will choose what it chooses. Neither you nor I can influence its path. It will be revealed to you when it is time for you to know."

"It *has* been revealed to me: that is what I know that you do not. It was revealed to Set. He and I had quite a… conversation. I know the end. You do not. So don't give me, of all people, my own lecture about the timing of the Earth's events," the Protector bellowed.

"'You are despicable in your person, and this office is too much for you, you lad, the flavor of whose mouth is still bad.'* We are finished, Protector," the being cried.

"Yes, we are." He turned to leave.

"Wait." A pause. "Since you already know the end, fate has seen fit to give you back your knowledge of future events, the same as you have had before. However, it comes with this warning: Interfere with fate's plans again, and you will cease to be, forever and eternally. Another will be called in your place. You will perish, unable to claim your spot as a member of the Powers That Be."

"So be it," the Protector stated, and left the room without another word.

***

The sun continued its struggle to light the sky to no avail. The shadows extinguished its light for the second day running. Newscasters and meteorologists explained the phenomenon with words like *eclipse* and *natural evolution*, but Rick knew better. He felt his thoughts being flooded with new information, information he should have already been given the time to sort through. With this flood of knowledge came unimportant details as well. Sorting out which visions were important and which ones were not was more difficult than he could have imagined. The future mingled with the thoughts of the present, and Rick saw the wedding. Cassi was attired in a black dress, much as she had been wearing the night she had met Dominique as the slayer for the first time. It moved upon her as a shadow, whispering soothing words in her ear to calm her nerves. Her blond hair was pulled up off her neck in a tight storm, overlooked by a threatening veil that hung loosely over her face, inviting the shadows to dance there as well. The entire outfit was accented by that glamorous necklace which shielded Cassi from the light. Lucas also chose black and dressed in somewhat the traditional manner with a dress suit and cape much like his father had worn every day of his life. Lucas accented his attire with a large Cobra, which hung tightly around his neck.

Rick could see and hear the ceremony in his mind. Cassi stood giving Lucas her rapt attention, while Lucas was so blinded by what he was gaining that he never paused to think of the repercussions—of the fact that he was ruining Cassi's life.

So it is with evil, Rick thought, *it would blind you with instant gratification—greed, gain, or power—with no thought of remorse. Only the light of truth can stop you from delivering yourself, or another, into the hands of darkness. It can only do this by bringing to your mind the value of what could be lost. Evil hides the value and leaves you with nothing but debt.*

Melanie raised herself out of her seat and approached the two. She took the weight of the Cobra off Lucas's shoulders and set it on the ground in a coiled heap between the two vampires. Her words echoed:

"The Cobra, the serpent—symbol of power and glory since the first serpent, our Master, tempted Eve and caused her downfall. That great fall has paved the way for us to be here today. That great fall was the beginning of our power. The light (try as it may), too, has a Master, a magic that shows the good the way to destruction—our destruction. Now who is winning? Now who has the power?"

The snake hissed.

"Strike, Master, give these thy servants thy blessing." Rick watched as the Cobra slithered over Cassi's feet, trapping her. It lifted its head and struck, filling the wound with venom. It then untwined itself and repeated the process with Lucas.

"You have been accepted by our Lord," Melanie said with a trembling voice. "To seal the marriage, Lucas must accept his bride!"

Rick struggled in his thoughts, the unbelievable playing in his head like a well-scripted movie. He watched as Lucas's face twisted and his fangs became exposed. Cassi lifted her veil and stepped to embrace him. Lucas pulled her body into him and plunged his icy teeth into her soft flesh. Cassi let out a cry and fell deeper into his arms. She dug her nails into his back, the pain almost unbearable.

This was the last scene that played on Rick's mind as the vision faded. The Protector was able to return to his clear, but overcrowded thoughts.

I must stop this, he thought. But as he stood to consult *Amun-Ra*, a horrible realization crossed his mind. It wasn't the future he was seeing, it was the present, and he was already too late.

***

"How was the ceremony, sister?" Nannette questioned Melanie as she entered the main cavern. "Excellent. All went according to plan."

"And the heir to the throne?" Sara asked, a short

stride behind Nannette.

Melanie smirked, "That should be a private matter to be reserved only between Lucas and his bride."

"You wallow in the thought of a power we can control as well. I know you do," Nannette retorted, straightening her back in a manner of confrontation.

Melanie's smirk turned into an open-mouthed grin. "The heir should be on its way soon."

"And yours, Melanie?"

"Mine, Dear?" she responded, resting her hand lightly on her stomach. "Oh, I suppose he shall make a powerful second."

CHAPTER TWENTY

Dominique gulped from the park's water fountain. Fatigued and discouraged, she crawled to the ground and lay on the grass. Her search for Cassi and Lucas had turned up nothing within the past few days, but Dominique knew that they must be somewhere around town. After all, who else could bring such evil that the sun couldn't rise. For some strange reason, Dominique couldn't help but think about the Protector's prophecy. Gazing at the stars, Dominique tried to remember the constellations she was taught as a kid. "Big Dipper," she whispered, "the Seven Sisters, Leo, and… no. *The sign in the sky*. It couldn't be. Could it?" Her mind and body betrayed her however, because before she could do anything with the information she had suddenly realized, it was pulled from her by a wave of sudden sleep.

***

Dominique woke abruptly to the sounds of snapping twigs in the nearby forest. Her eyes blurred because she sat up so suddenly, but focused quickly on a dark figure emerging from the trees. It walked toward her and froze, aware that it was being watched. It hesitated momentarily, and then again began a noisy walk toward her, materializing into a dominant figure as it grew closer.

"It's a bit past curfew," the figure spoke. Officer Allred loomed above Dominique.

"Curfew?"

"The town has been put on alert. An emergency situation, the mayor calls it."

"Sorry. What time is it anyway?" Dominique asked, rubbing her eyes.

"Just after midnight. I'd suggest you run home. There have been some strange things going on in these woods, and with the crazy mornings we've been having lately, all the weirdos seem to be out."

"Yeah, you're talking to one of them," Dominique chuckled.

Kendra laughed and eased her stance a little. "Do you want a ride?"

"Nah, I'm a big girl," Dominique whispered.

"Well, good night then."

"Hey wait," Dominique said. "I remember a while ago, when all this started, you came to visit us, to speak with a guy named Rick."

Kendra turned back to her, "I thought you looked

familiar. You must have been one of the ones in the back room while I was talking to him."

Dominique tensed. "How did you remember that?"

Kendra laughed, "I'm pretty observant."

"Well, when you spoke to him, Rick, I mean, you seemed pretty upset. Do you remember if he told you anything about Cassi, no matter how insignificant?"

"Just that he had many secrets, and that we were meant to cross paths. Honestly, I think Rick's an okay guy. I misjudged him. He's sure surrounded by a lot of bad luck though. A lot of deaths happening in that group of his. You're lucky you got away. I don't think he's responsible, but it sure is strange, ya know?"

"Yeah," Dominique stated softly. "Cynthia was my best friend."

Kendra could have kicked herself for bringing it up. "Hey," she said, trying to lift Dominique's spirits, "sorry about her. That really was a tragedy. But you know, the universe has a funny way with things. That girl, Cassi? She's all right. I know she must have been your friend too, and you don't need to worry about her anymore. Looks like she just ran off for a while. I just saw her and that boyfriend of hers over at the church on Pine Street; they were breaking curfew too. Guess they just wanted to make their peace with God before they headed home."

Dominique smiled. "Thanks, maybe I'll go see them; it's been a while."

"Well, I doubt they're still there. I told them they needed to head home, and I suggest you do the same."

"Thanks, officer."

***

The Catholic church was cold, but its atmosphere was different from the stale air that crawled along the earth. Lucas and Cassi stood in front of Mother Mary, in awe of the deserted building.

"Looks like they cleaned it up," Lucas said. Plastic now covered the shattered windows, and the broken pews had all been removed, leaving the nicely polished floor empty. The only thing left in the room was the statue of Mary, her piercing black eyes and extending arms ready to embrace whatever good was left in the world. At the base of the statue were flowers. Dozens of white rose petals littered the ground at Mary's feet. Cassi bent over them, breathing in their fragrance. She touched the silky flowers to feel their softness.

"The slayer must have put these here," Cassi said respectfully. "This is where you laid her friend?"

"Yes," Lucas said, approaching Cassi from behind, caressing her shoulders.

"It's beautiful. Perhaps we should show our respect. Would that not be the polite thing to do?"

"Ah, see, you're learning well. Courtesy is important. We vampires are always polite. There are daisies growing in a field not too far from here. We could pick some and come back."

"You go. I wish to stay."

Lucas pulled her up to meet him and kissed her lightly on the cheek. "I'll be back soon."

"I'll be waiting, as I always will."

Lucas smiled and turned. Cassi heard his footsteps

slowly fade as he walked across the wooden floor. The door softly clicked as it closed behind him.

Cassi sat, folding her legs beneath her. She was dressed in the outfit that Lucas had given her as her first gift—khaki pants that tied at the waist and the lavender shirt that hugged her body. She sat admiring the beauty around her, the roses that Mary seemed to hold in her hand, and the petals that fell from them embracing Mary's feet. It was an empowering vision.

The door creaked as it opened behind her, and Cassi heard slow steps approaching. "That was fast. Did you get the flowers?" Cassi asked, turning to her lover. Only it wasn't him. "Dominique," Cassi whispered defiantly. "It has been a long time."

"Not long enough by my watch," Dominique answered, eyeing Cassi in a way that made her feel uncomfortable.

"You look well."

"As do you."

"I should let you know that I am expecting Lucas back at any moment."

"No, he is picking wild flowers. That is what you have done to him you know, turned the Prince of Darkness into a pansy. Maybe he'll just stay out in that field forever. Besides, I hope he does come back. The sooner the better. Pushing a stake into his heart will be a definite pleasure."

"Is that what you have come here to do?" Cassi asked wryly, "Destroy us?"

"I have come to fight for good."

"Liar. You have come to take out a personal grudge.

You left the circle. You left Rick, James, everything you believed in, everything good. You fight for yourself. Rick fights for good. James fought for good."

"Fought?"

"Oh, didn't you know? James was killed last night. He betrayed his own family, and then they betrayed him."

"James's family is dead."

"That's what James believed too, and that belief killed him. Isn't it strange how an erroneous belief can kill someone? I find that fascinating. What do you believe in, Dominique?"

Dominique's mind began to spin, but she quickly regained her composure. She had come to complete a task, and she wasn't going to let anything get in her way. "Don't play your little mind games with me. I'm a slayer, trained to hunt and kill your kind. I've studied your tricks; they won't work on me."

"So you're not going to answer the question?"

Dominique answered smugly, "Do you know what I believe? I believe you have just spoken some of your last words. How does it feel to know that you wasted them on me?"

Cassi smirked, "Just as James's belief was his undoing, that belief, too, shall be yours."

"It's hard to believe: here I am with *the sign in the sky* and all you can do is mutter about beliefs. What's your real name anyway?"

"You already know."

"Yes I do know," Dominique sneered, pausing briefly before adding, "Cassiopeia."

Dominique lunged, Cassi blocked. Both were surprised at the force to which they were subjected. Dominique followed with a high right, which caught Cassi off guard and sent her crashing into a nearby wall. "Come on, you're a vampire! You can do better than that."

Cassi's face twisted as anger welled up inside her. She stared down at a gash in her leg that was quickly growing red with blood. "You ripped my pants," she said, following with a blow that sent Dominique skidding on the polished floor to the other end of the building. Dominique quickly recovered and bounded back to her feet.

"Bite me, vamp!" she cried.

Cassi grinned. "With pleasure."

Lucas was making his way up the walk when he heard a loud crash, followed by a hiss and a laugh. He dropped the daisies he had been carrying and sprinted to the door. "Cassi!" he yelled, as he realized the heavy wooden doors were locked. He pounded his fists on the door helplessly. Finally he punched the door as hard as he could. He winced in pain as the door splintered, and his broken hand chewed through the wood. Ignoring the pain, he grabbed the inner lock and thrust it open. He now stood in an inner foyer, one door away from his beloved. He was about to use his good hand to break the lock on that door, when a voice spoke behind him.

"Allow me," it said. "We will need that other hand of yours."

Lucas whirled around and caught the eyes of the Protector. With a wave of his hand the door swung open. Lucas looked confused, but didn't stop to think about why this being would help him. He rushed into the room, scanning it for his love. She was struggling in the middle of the room with Dominique. Cassi defended herself magnificently, and Lucas paused, beginning to wonder if he should interfere.

"Wait," Rick said. "We need to talk."

Lucas turned to the Protector with a growl. There were two battles waging around him, one with his love, and the other within himself. The evil inside him told him to hate this being of light, but something inside his head whispered that he needed to hear what this good entity had to say. As if in a trance, Lucas followed Rick into a shadowed corner.

"Why am I still alive?" he asked the Protector angrily. "And why am I talking to you instead of saving Cassi?"

"We don't have time for silly questions. Just listen. I do believe you are familiar with a legend your father often repeated to you as a child. It goes something like this:

> *A loud moaning cry heard from heaven to hell*
> *Escaping the aching lips of the just,*
> *A sorrowful groan from the one known as He*
> *When a cackle of chaos from the darkness fell.*

> *The eyes of mother, twinkling in the sky*
> *Her belly soon swells, and sealed is her fate.*
> *Her eyes grow dim, her heart hungry for blood,*
> *For the baby she bears is near its birth date.*

His coming will mark the hold of black roots,
Its disease will spread to new heights of the sky,
Blackness will blow and ripple the faith,
One may make light prevail; many will try.

A slayer be born, the world to defend,
Darkness and domination will soon after part.
The tyranny silenced as a new power purges,
Puts an end to the life of the Head through the heart.

"Yes, the legend that speaks of my Cassi and her child," Lucas spouted. "And we are winning!"

"Do you know why the witches killed your father, Lucas?"

"He was attempting to kill my bride, Protector. He was allowing good to win."

"Why would he do that? Did you ever consider that perhaps your father knew something greater than you can imagine, information that I now possess? Would you like to know what that information was? What that information is?"

"Why should I believe anything you say?"

"I am light, good; I do not lie."

Lucas paused. "What could you possibly know that I do not?"

The Protector smiled. "I was asked a similar question recently, by fate itself. What I know is that fate has finally determined an outcome to more than this battle. It has determined an outcome to the war."

"Tell me."

"Brother... neither one of us will win. Fate started this battle because it was bored with the planet, bored with humanity. This war was to end the world. But now, fate has changed its mind. It has decided that the world is to continue. Dominique's role in this plan is greater than all of ours. It is because of her that they have decided to continue this planet. She surprised them when she left my circle, and again when she maintained her integrity. They realized, then, that there are people here who can still entertain them. They called off the war. That means, Lucas, that if fate has its way, tonight will end in a draw, and the only way for the both of us to win, is for your bride to die."

Lucas squinted and turned his head as if the words hit him harder than any other blow he had ever received in his entire existence. "Please, no!" he begged, then realizing what he truly felt, he stated without hesitation, "I love her."

"An interesting truth. A twist you did not foresee, but your father did."

"The legend says that you are the one who changes the course of fate and makes light prevail. Do so if you must. Destroy me. Destroy the witches. Just please, please, do not destroy her."

"Lucas. Boy. I cannot interfere. You see... you have been misinformed. *I* am not the one who has the power to make light prevail."

Lucas's thoughts were suddenly perfectly clear. "My father was trying to save... me!"

"So it would seem."

Lucas nodded to the Protector, who smiled weakly,

and turned to the fighting. Dominique now had a stake in hand, ready to strike Cassi the moment the opportunity arose. Lucas looked at Mary, her forgiving eyes staring into his. He held his head defiantly and began a slow pace toward his love.

At that moment the balance in the battle turned, and Dominique was favored. She pushed Cassi to the center of the hall and turned to her exposed heart. The world moved in slow motion as the war came to a close. Dominique raised her stake, poised, perfectly balanced, ready to strike. Lucas approached slowly. Dominique's hand came down, and Lucas lunged. Cassi saw his body blur her vision, and an incredible tug tore flesh from her neck. Lucas fell to the ground staring up at Cassi.

"I will always love you," he whispered. Cassi knelt at his side, noticing a wooden point penetrating his back, squarely through his heart.

"No!" Cassi cried, embracing him. She laid her head on his chest and listened to his shallow attempts to inhale. The tears that fell from her eyes mixed with dust, causing muddy spots to appear on the necklace that Lucas had torn from her neck.

"It is finished!" the Protector cried aloud, a tear of light falling softly down his cheek. It slid off his face and struck the ground, releasing an incredibly brilliant force. In this circle of power, Cassi heard the Protector repeat the following words:

> The Osiris Ani saith: "Hail, thou god Aniu! Hail, thou god Pehreri, who dwellest in thy hall, the Great God. Grant thou that her soul may come to

her from any place wherein it may be. Even if it would tarry, let her soul be brought unto her from any place wherein it may be. Thou findest the Eye of Horus standing by thee like unto those beings who resemble Osiris, who never lie down in death. Let not the Osiris Ani, whose word is truth, lie down dead among those who lie in Anu, the land wherein souls are joined to their bodies in thousands. Let her have possession of her Ba-soul and of her Spirit-soul, and let my word be truth with it, the Ba-soul, in every place wherein it may be. Observe then, O ye guardians of Heaven, her soul, wherever it may be. Even if it would tarry, cause thou her Ba-soul to see her body. Thou shalt find the Eye of Horus standing by thee like the Watchers."*

In the light, Cassi felt a strange sensation as she lost her fangs. They fell from her mouth, piercing the stones of the necklace. The anger that caused her face to contort vanished, and her bruises and cuts healed. In the incredible light that surrounded her, a small doorway opened and Cassi felt her soul being ripped from purgatory. Her heart kicked to life, and she became warm as renewed life and strength entered into her like a fountain of light amidst the desert of darkness.

The sun rose that morning.

CHAPTER TWENTY-ONE

It was raining, but the sun shone through the clouds, and the rain was the kind that brought with it the fresh scent of renewal.

"Here it is, the legend that Lucas spoke of. It is all about you, your life, and your death, as the Powers That Be see fit to have it."

Rain rolled off her face and fell on the pages like the tears that she had not been able to control. "I don't understand," Cassi whispered as Rick placed his warm arm around her shoulders.

He smiled. "Your child is very important. Whether on the dark side or the light, your child will accomplish great things. You see, if the child were raised with Lucas as the father, he would grow to be the most powerful vampire this world would ever know. Now that things have... changed, *when* you have a child, *she* will be a great slayer, so you must prepare yourself now. Having a slayer for a child is not easy; but if anyone can do it, you can."

"The necklace?"

"The necklace protected you from my power. It was the only way Set knew you would stay evil, by taking away your choice. Vampires have rules, and with you, they broke them. They tricked you into becoming one of them. That is why I had the power to change you back. Set knew that since they removed your choice, I would have the power to do so, so he crafted the necklace with the help of the witches to trap you into the evil they needed you to be."

"The legend makes sense now," Cassi nodded, as Rick closed *Amun-Ra*. She remained quiet for a moment, then said, "I remember being in... so many places... at once. When I heard Lucas's voice calling to me, he used your name. If those words came from the *Book of the Dead*, then what I don't understand is..." she paused, "it's *your* power that allows vampires to exist."

"Interesting how fate balances the universe, isn't it? I thought you would have learned that by now," he answered. "Yes, in theory, you are right. The incantation was originally used by the Egyptian priests at a funeral to aid the soul in returning to paradise. It was changed by Judas, to awaken those he had killed."

"And the spell you used to return me to life—that too was found in the *Book of the Dead*."

"Do you honestly not understand that books as powerful as *Amun-Ra* or the *Book of the Dead* would have included spells from the other? The incantation I used was originally written by Ra, but later included in the *Book of the Dead* so that evil, too, could use it—if they were worthy. The power, in the hands of good, does great things. Likewise, great destruction comes from that same power in the hands of darkness."

Cassi thought for another minute, understanding crossing her face. For a brief moment she remembered that James had once taught her something similar. Now that he was gone, that memory seemed so distant. Finally she added another question, "What about Dominique? I owe her so much."

"You owe her nothing; it is part of her calling. She sends her love and asks your forgiveness. She's on a bus on its way to Seattle right now. There is work to be done there," Rick said.

Cassi nodded silently.

Rick gave Cassi a look of comfort. "He loved you; I hope you know that."

"He gave his life for me," Cassi whispered, tears again springing to her eyes.

"You will see him again."

"How? He was a vampire. He chose his life."

"Did he choose? He was the façade of shadows, their pretense, veneer, face, and outward show, nothing more. They were proud of him, as they should have been. Now, you should be. He chose you. That's the important thing. Even though he chose his life, he also chose his fate. Did you know that sacrifice, in its purest form, can redeem a bad choice? It can't erase it; it can't undo what was done, but redemption is more about paying a debt than forgiving it. Now I know that isn't much comfort, but you must know that I will save him a place... a place with you."

"And you? What about you?" Cassi interrupted.

Rick was pleased. "Cassiopeia, that has yet to be determined. Yet whether I'm there, or whether I'm not, it doesn't matter. All that is important is your love. Now here," he said, pushing a red rose into her hands. "Go," he continued, pointing to the cathedral.

Cassi nodded her head. "Before I do, there is something we need to talk about."

"Okay."

"When you changed me back, I saw something."

Rick grinned. "I cannot explain to you your vision. When I use my gifts on someone, they usually play a part in one of my memories. The females, in particular, always play the role of my mother. She teaches them a lesson, a private lesson, about their lives. Whatever she taught you is for you alone. I saw glimpses of Dominique's vision, of Kendra's too, but I guess my mother intended for yours to be extremely private, as I saw none of it. Don't worry, you'll figure it out."

"She told me you'd say that."

"*She* told you?"

"That's right. Horus, I didn't play a part in what I saw. I was me. I spoke with your mother, and she told me some things… some things I already knew. When I was being changed into a vampire, as I drank from the wrist of that monster, I learned things. I still know them. When I saw you, as you tried to save me, I heard your thoughts. You were practically screaming them at me. You were so upset that I was being changed, but your reason… the reason you were upset… well… it confirmed something to me. You have feelings for me. You were more upset over the thought that we could never be with each other again, than you were over the fact that I lost my life. You were concerned for my life in a way you have never been before. Was that the first time you had ever put your own value and wants over another's?"

"I'm sorry. I value your life more than my own; you know that. And yes, perhaps the reason for that is because I was upset over losing you, more so than any other person I've ever lost."

"So you *do* have feelings for me?"

"It is against my rules to love. I made that mistake that night. The way I acted when you were killed… that is exactly why it is against my rules to love. I blamed the slayers, when really I was hurt. I am resolved to never make that mistake again."

"Mistake? Your mother told me to tell you to throw the rulebook out the window and live your life. She told me you are entitled to that much."

"I cannot. I don't know how."

"I will help you," Cassi said, moving toward him.

Rick put his hand gently to her lips, and with tears of pain in his eyes stated, "Your heart belongs to another."

Cassi took his hand in hers. "Then let me borrow yours."

They shared a kiss. It was, for Cassi's soul, her first kiss. Something within her ignited: a will to live, a will to do what she was called to do, a will to love again.

When the kiss ended, Cassi stood from the park bench they sat on. She walked across the clearing in the rain, the cathedral in sight. She turned, "When will I see you…" she glanced around.

The Protector was gone.

Cassi allowed herself a weak smile before she turned back to her walk. When she reached the cathedral, light was streaming through the newly installed stained glass windows. One of the new windows depicted a sun rising over the mountains, or was it setting? That remained unknown. Cassi approached the Virgin Mary, whose expression of love Cassi now felt deeply. The red rose she carried fell at the statue's feet, and as she turned to leave, she resolved, that for her, the sun was rising.

ACKNOWLEDGMENTS

All my real-life Sexy Slayers:
Dominique Winther
Cynthia Phimmasone
Kendra Allred
Casseopia Bergman
Melanie McKenzie
Sara Doty
Nanette Stam
James Siale

And Annalee Reed, for the Prophecy

*These passages were taken from and include translations from the Legend of Osiris and *The Book of the Coming Forth by Day*, colloquially known as *The Book of the Dead*. Some words have been edited to fit the story line. Special thanks to www.touregypt.net.

CAN'T GET ENOUGH?

See how my writing style has changed over the last ten years by reading the Prologue to my new series, immediately following this page.

DEATH OF THE BODY

CROSSING DEATH:
BOOK ONE

"This is a fully realized world that rivals **Anne Rice** or **William Gibson**."
~Christopher M. Jimenez (SinfulCelluloid.com)

"Death of the Body is a roller-coaster ride that will leave you **questioning reality, religion, and everything you thought you knew**. Be ready to lose yourself in this amazing story."
~Rebecca Ethington, author of the Imdalind series

PROLOGUE

I watched in disbelief as blood seeped through my fingers and dripped, thick as syrup, to the ground. I heard each drop thud against the ground beneath me. The echo in my ears beat louder than any drum. For the first time in my ten years of life, I cursed the connection I had with the planet. I cursed it for its betrayal. I cursed it because, with every drop of blood that spilled, the planet felt my pain and mimicked my screams with its own bleating sound that bounced around inside my already spinning head.

My legs were weak and my knees buckled but I didn't dare let my hands loosen from around the wound in my stomach. I caught the weight of my fall with my face. I rolled onto my side in order to breathe. Pain surged as the ragged edges of my wound rubbed together. I felt every last severed nerve. They were all on fire.

Blood poured quickly. Worse than seeing it, I could feel it, hot and sticky in a pool beneath me. My stomach retched but it would hurt to throw up so I tried to force down the feeling. Bile came up anyway. I turned my head and choked it out. The rusty taste left in my mouth was so sour it made my eyes water. I cried uncontrollably, feeling ashamed of myself.

I wished for the comfort of my mother and father. I longed for the company of my two best friends. It was ironic that I'd just had a conversation about death with them a day ago.

As I lay sobbing on the ground, the thought that I was going to die became more and more real. Already my blood was soaking back into the earth that I loved so much. I thought of the lessons that taught me not to fear death. I had been taught that death was a return to the larger conscious mind that is nature. This awareness made my people who they were and gave us our unique gifts.

I was afraid anyway. The thought of dying was much more terrifying now than when it was taught to me by the Elders.

The Elders. The Elders who were either dead or enslaved. The Elder who betrayed us all and who did this to me.

Rage: pure, blazing, and blinding in its fury. I was too enraged to even notice that I could feel anything besides pain. Rage boiled inside me as blood boiled from my stomach and I realized it was based in two other emotions: hate and disbelief.

Then something cold and wet hit me between the eyes. I rolled onto my back and stared into the dark and threatening clouds. Another something hit the back of my hand, and I lifted it (was my arm always this heavy?). A drop of rain mingled with my blood.

I had never experienced rain before. It never rained here—at least not in my lifetime. Rain was for when the world was angry, when its powers had been abused and the balance of life had been disrupted.

But wasn't I angry? And wasn't I connected to the planet? Didn't I understand its moods and feelings? Why wouldn't it then understand *me*? In my delirium this seemed to make sense, and the large flash of lightning that then split the sky seemed to confirm my thoughts. The flash was blinding, and I didn't have enough energy to be startled by the fact that my vision remained nothing but the same bright white light.

I shivered as cold crept into me; it didn't help that I was lying in a chilling pool of blood. The rain picked up. I was nearly soaked through, but was too weak and numb to move. At least the pain was starting to slip away. I could only imagine how blue my fingertips must have looked. They felt like ice.

After the pain was gone, the fear began to fade. All the tension in my body went with it. Cold as I was, I started to feel strangely comfortable. I could feel the earth beneath me, supporting me, soft and gentle. My mom used to hold me like this.

When I realized the rage was slipping, I cried out. I wanted to keep it alive within me. I wanted to be angry and upset. I wanted to be angry because feeling an emotion—any emotion—was better than accepting death.

As the rage faded further, I thought I heard distant laughter. How could anyone be happy now? How could they laugh as I lay here, a mangled mess? It took me a minute to remember that just because the earth could feel my pain didn't mean everyone else could too— especially not the outsiders.

Their voices were getting louder and nearer. When they suddenly stopped, I heard a gasp. Mustering the last of my strength, I reached toward the voices.

"Please," I tried to say, but it came out as barely

more than a groan.

"Get a doctor!" a woman's voice commanded. I felt slight vibrations through the earth as somebody ran away. The woman who spoke came over and kneeled next to me. I wasn't too far gone to feel surprise. I imagined I was a frightening sight. I expected her to keep her distance, so my eyes widened when she took my hand in hers. She was warm, but trembling.

"What did this to you, child?" Her voice shook but was full of compassion and concern.

"Magic." I couldn't tell if I actually said the word or just thought it.

As I repeated the word over and over in my mind, the rage dissipated and the light began to dim. A part of me was upset that I'd let the rage go but I was too exhausted to call it back. I welcomed the darkness now. The woman at my side was saying something but her words made no sense to me. Far easier to hear was the heartbeat of the earth. I wanted to soothe the earth's tremors caused by the pain and fear it felt for me, but I couldn't. As my breathing slowed, memories of the past day flashed into my mind. They were of the events that led up to my death, when all this started. It seemed like a lifetime ago. Who would have known it would only be one long day that would lead me here, lying on the ground, spilling blood?

ABOUT THE AUTHOR

Hi, I'm Rick. Here is the "About the Author" that was at the end of the original edition of *Façade of Shadows*:

Rick Chiantaretto graduated from Weber State University where he studied computer science and English. He wrote as a fiction columnist for *Scribe and Quill Magazine*, and was a regular volunteer at the Utah Humanities Council (where his favorite work was helping with the Great Salt Lake Book Festival). Rick is a writer of horror and dark fantasy, with a flair for satire. A native of West Valley City, Utah, Rick stays busy with his love for technology and works as a computer scientist—that is, until he becomes a best-selling author. He can be contacted at his website: www.rickthauthor.com

STALK RICK

Official Website: www.ricktheauthor.com
Facebook: www.facebook.com/rickchiantaretto
Goodreads: www.goodreads.com/ricktheauthor
Twitter: @RickTheAuthor

Also available by Rick Chiantaretto

Death of the Body (Crossing Death #1)

See a mistake?

As perfect as I want every book to be, something was missed. If you find an editing problem, please don't hesitate to email me at rick@rickchiantaretto.com with the mistake. I would love to reward you with some swag, free books, or maybe even eternal life (especially if your name is Mary. Did I mention how much I love a good Bloody Mary?).